I0607573

Jake Stellar

When Death Returns

By

Rodney Riesel

Published by Island Holiday Publishing

East Greenbush, NY

ISBN: 978-0-9971149-0-4

First Edition

Special thanks to:

Pamela Guerriere

Kevin Cook

Cover Design by:

Connie Fitsik

To learn about my other books friend me at

https://www.facebook.com/rodneyriesel

For Brenda,
Kayleigh, Ethan
& Peyton

Chapter One

Bree pulled a pound of frozen bacon out the freezer and dropped it on the countertop next to the stove. The clunk when it hit caused me to look up from my Sunday funnies. She was watching for my reaction. She had asked me to take the bacon out of the freezer and stick it in the fridge the night before.

I sucked air in through my clenched teeth. "I forgot to take that out of the freezer last night, didn't I?"

"Yup," Bree answered. "*And* the garbage is still overflowing."

I glanced over at the stainless steel trash can. The lid was propped open by an empty soup can and a Styrofoam to go container. "If you push the garbage down I think a little more will fit."

"If you take *out* the garbage, like I asked you to yesterday, a *lot* more will fit."

"I forgot … sorry."

Bree folded her arms in front of her and leaned against the countertop. "Do you think you're too busy to do it now, Jake?" she asked.

I raised the newspaper a little and said, "I have to find out what trouble Marmaduke gets himself into," then I flashed her an ear-to-ear grin.

She didn't laugh, she didn't even smile. Instead she made her way over to the trash can and began removing the bag herself. I knew what she was doing. It was her same old trick. She starts doing something that she has asked me to do, and then I get up and do it. If she was really going to do it herself she would have just done it, not wait till I'm in the room, bitch about it, and *then* start doing it herself. We've lived on Hillside Drive, in North Myrtle Beach, for well over ten years now and I've never once seen her take out the garbage, nor have I ever seen her mow the lawn. But I have seen her *pretend* to start doing things like that several times, in an attempt to get me off of my ass and moving.

I watched her struggle with the bag for a second, and even watched as she tore the side of it. I wonder what she would do if I didn't get up and just went back to reading my paper. Would she actually take out the garbage? Would I actually ever hear the end of it?

I slid my chair back from the table. "Here, hon, Let me get that for you."

She was still manhandling the Hefty sack as if it contained a body. "No, you just sit there and read your paper."

"I got it."

Bree stepped back and I pulled the bag from the can with ease and tied it closed.

"Thanks," she said.

"Welx," I answered, and carried the bag out to the garage.

When I returned to the kitchen Bree was standing in front of the TV watching the weather.

"Is there anything else you would like me to do?" I asked.

"Yes. Get your running stuff on so we can get a few miles in. According to the weather nerds. It looks like the rain is going to stop for an hour or so. I would like to go and get back before it starts again."

"Yes, ma'am," I responded with a salute, and made my way down the hall to the bedroom. I didn't feel like running, but I knew I would be glad I did.

I grabbed my red running shorts with the white stripe down the side and a black T-shirt and began removing my pajama bottoms. "Are you making breakfast when we get back?" I called out.

"That's why I wanted you to take the bacon out of the freezer," she yelled back.

I wonder if that's a yes or a no, I thought.

After I finished dressing, I put on my running shoes and joined Bree in the driveway.

The sun was doing its best to shine through the scattering of clouds and steam was rising from the hot wet blacktop and sidewalk. It was humid.

I squatted and put my hands flat on the wet pavement, stretched my right leg back and then my left leg. When I got up I rubbed my hands together to remove the small bits of gravel. "I love that smell after it rains," I commented.

Bree took a deep breath. "Me, too."

"How far did you want to run?" I asked.

"Four miles sound good? I don't want to get rained on."

"Roger that. So then, pancakes with the bacon?"

Bree stood on one leg, pulling her ankle up to her butt. There was the hint of a smile. "Yes."

"I love you," I said.

"I love *you*."

Bree took off running; I followed. My cell phone, which was clipped to my shorts, began to vibrate. I stopped and answered it. "Yeah?"

It was Dill Perkins. "Jake, we got one. Outrigger Road, behind Krispy Kreme."

"Give me fifteen minutes."

Bree was already walking back toward me. "Everything okay?" she asked.

"Fraid not, honey bun, I gotta go in."

She pushed up on her tiptoes and gave me a kiss. "Be careful."

I nodded. She turned and I smacked her on the ass. "Run a couple miles for me."

Chapter Two

I took a left off of North Kings Highway onto Thirteenth Avenue South, drove halfway down the block and parked my black Ford F-150 in the side lot of Krispy Kreme. I instinctually glanced at the big neon HOT NOW sign in the front window, it wasn't glowing red, and the place was dark inside. Still, my mouth watered at the thought of biting into that glazed goodness. Food of the Gods, in my book.

There were several patrol cars, an ambulance, an emergency vehicle from the fire department, and the medical examiner's van already on the scene. The entire rear parking lot was sectioned off with plastic yellow CRIME SCENE DO NOT CROSS tape and a few of the uniformed officers stood around the perimeter to intimidate onlookers.

Detective Dill Perkins met me in the parking lot. "What do we have?" I asked.

Perkins flipped open the notepad he kept in his back pocket. "Female. Paige Samuels. Twenty-three. Student ID from Coastal Carolina and her driver's license were in her back pocket. License lists her address as 1112 Coral Sand Drive."

We walked toward the cluster of first responders. "Where's the body?"

"Dumpster."

I shook my head. "Jesus Christ."

"The assistant manager, Craig Patterson, found the body when he took out the garbage ... around seven this morning."

As we approached the dumpster, Detective Gwen Lawrence walked around from behind it. She was a tall drink of water, about five foot eight. The rim of the dumpster stood at least four inches above her head.

"Dumpsters almost six feet tall," I commented. "Does Patterson always look inside when he throws in a bag of garbage?"

"I asked him that same question."

"Great minds."

"Patterson said he threw the bag into the dumpster, like he always does, and it got hung up on the edge. He said he climbed up to dislodge it. That's when he looked inside and found Ms. Samuels."

Gwen nodded to me as she removed the blue latex gloves she was wearing. I nodded back. She joined the medical examiner at the rear of his van.

"Craig Patterson?" I asked, motioning toward the

young man on the other side of the parking lot. He sat on the cement curb with his back against the concrete column of a light pole. His legs were pulled up to his chest and his chin rested on his knees. He couldn't have been more that nineteen.

"That's him," Perkins informed me.

"You told him to stick around?"

"Yeah. He's asked me twice if he can open the shop."

"Might as well tell him the shop's gonna be opening a little late today, maybe around noon." I inspected the exterior of the building and noticed two security cameras mounted under the soffit. One pointed at the side parking lot, the other aimed at the rear. "Also, have him give you his manager's phone number. Let's get him down here so we can have a look at what those security cameras may have recorded."

Perkins started toward the kid, paused and turned. "There's three other employees waiting in their cars in the front parking lot. They were supposed to work this morning. Should I tell them to take off?"

"Tell them to sit tight. I'll get to them in a minute."

"You got it, Jake."

I turned and made my way over to join Gwen and the ME. I quickly looked Gwen up and down. Something about her seemed different.

Gwen caught me mid-gaze *"What?"* she demanded.

"Nothing," I answered.

Thomas Powers had been with the Horry County Coroner's Office for at least as long as I had been with the North Myrtle Beach Police Department. He was barely over five feet tall and looked up at Gwen as he spoke to her. His hair was light-colored and parted on the side. He had a very neat appearance, and whenever I saw him I was reminded of a third grader waiting to get his class picture taken. He looked far too young to have the job he had, for as long as he did. Someone told me once that he graduated medical school at the age of seventeen. I don't know if they were pulling my leg, but since then I've called him Doogie Powers ... behind his back, of course.

"What can you tell me, Tom?" I asked.

"Time of death is between 1:30 AM and 3:30 AM. Cause of death is blunt force trauma to the back of the skull. She was killed somewhere else and dumped here within an hour of her death."

"Any sign of the murder weapon?" I asked.

"No sign of anything, Jake," Gwen answered. "No weapon, no tire marks, no footprints. It rained pretty damn hard last night and early this morning. Not ideal weather for preserving crime scenes."

Tom stared at Gwen as she spoke. He seemed a little irritated that *she* answered my question instead of him. When she finished he said, "*Anyway*, the murder weapon was probably metal ... approximately one inch in diameter."

"Any sign of sexual assault?" I asked.

"Not as far as I can tell, but I won't know for sure until I get her on the table."

I heard a car pull up and I turned around to see Avis Lint, my intrepid partner, clambering from an unmarked car in a process roughly akin to trying to thread a needle with an egg. The three of us watched as he waddled across the parking lot. "What do we got, Jake?" he asked.

"Dead girl in a dumpster."

He winced. "Christ! Sounds like a headline outta the *New York Post*."

"There's something else, Jake," Gwen said, and motioned for me to follow her. Lint followed too.

Someone had placed a six-foot step ladder next to the dumpster. Gwen climbed up the ladder and I put my hands on the top of the dumpster and pulled myself up to look inside.

There she was ... someone's little girl, thrown away in a dumpster like the rest of the garbage. Mom and dad probably didn't even know she was missing yet. She lay there on her back, her arms over her head, and her legs together, turned to the side. She wore faded denim shorts, white Nikes with a blue Swoosh, a blue T-shirt, and a light brown leather jacket.

As I stared down at her I felt three or four drops of cold rain hit the back of my neck. I looked up at the dark gray clouds scudding overhead and then back into the dumpster at her. I felt a chill crawl up my back.

"You see her eyes, Jake?" Gwen asked.

It sounded like a dumb question. "Yeah. They're open."

"They're not just open. They've been glued open."

I looked closer. "Shit."

"Yeah. Tom says he thinks it's Krazy Glue, or something similar. He said it looks like they were glued open while she was still alive."

I shuddered, and hoped Gwen thought it was from the cold rain, which was starting to come down a little harder. I watched as rain droplets smacked the poor kid's face. I jumped down from the edge of the dumpster. "Get her out of there and let's find her parents."

"Will do," said Gwen. "And Jake?"

"Yeah?"

"You don't have to play seen-it-all, desensitized cop with me."

I grinned knowingly. Gwen could read me like a comic book.

I walked past Lint and he grabbed my arm. "What did she say about her eyes?" he asked. He had a sense of awareness in his eyes and a look of concern on is face that wasn't normal for him.

I leaned in closer to him so as not to be overheard. "Gwen said the girl's eyelids had been glued open."

Lint's eyes slowly left mine and he gazed off in the distance over my shoulder. "The *Garbage Man*," he whispered.

Chapter Three

I had one of the uniforms drive Lint's car back to the station so he could ride with me in my truck. We pulled out of the Krispy Kreme parking lot and I immediately turned to him and asked, "Okay, Lint, who or what the hell is the *Garbage Man*?"

Lint was fidgeting with the seat belt, trying to get it around his big belly. "Forget it," he mumbled, and let the belt retract. "He was one of North Myrtle Beach's first recorded serial killers."

"First recorded? Jesus, how many have there been?"

"I don't know. A few, I guess."

"When was this Garbage Man active? How many victims?"

"Four victims. We're talking almost twenty-five years ago, Jake. Before your time"

"But the guy you're talking about would still be in jail," I pointed out.

"Yeah, if we had caught him."

"Wait, you're telling me this *Garbage Man* guy is still out there?"

"As far as we know," Lint replied. "It was the fall of ninety-five, the first few weeks of October. Some guy raped and killed four college girls. One a week, if I remember correctly. The son of a bitch glued open their eyelids so they couldn't close their eyes while they were being assaulted. They had to witness every terrifying second. God, what a scumbag! When he was finished with them, he dumped the bodies in a dumpster, hence the name the *Garbage Man*."

"Clever," I said. "The newspapers seem to have a knack for making *anyone* famous."

"One more grisly tidbit. Before he dumped the bodies he bashed in their skulls. The ME at the time said he probably used an aluminum bat."

I pulled my truck into the parking lot of the North Myrtle Beach Police Station and parked. "I guess the first thing we better do is tell Captain Stein what you just told me," I said as we got out. "No one else has been here as long as you, so I'm sure no one else has made the connection yet."

As we made our way to the door, Lint asked, "Did you eat breakfast this morning?"

"No," I answered.

"Me neither."

"You could afford to skip breakfast, Lint," I

observed with a pointed glance at his belly. Then I looked at mine. It was starting to spill over my belt a little since I had fallen off of my health kick. "Suppose I could, too."

Lint snorted. "Yeah, the corporation's growing, like my old man used to say."

I was in no mood for Lint's ribbing. "Your belly may be a corporation, Lint, but mine's just a mom and pop store. Come on, let's get cracking. We'll see about breakfast later. Maybe."

I walked directly to my desk and opened the top drawer. I removed my pistol from its holster, placed it inside the drawer, and pushed it closed. I glanced over at Lint, who was doing the same thing at his desk. When he shut his drawer he looked back over his shoulder at me. I nodded toward Captain Stein's office door and we both headed in that direction.

CAPT. MERLE STEIN, the glass panel in the door read. I rapped on the glass with my knuckles once and went in, Lint followed.

Merle removed his reading glasses as we entered. "Good news, I hope," he said.

There was rarely a *good morning* with Merle, or a *how's your day,* and we were used to it.

I pushed the door closed. Lint took a seat on the dark leather sofa across from Merle's desk. I sat on the sofas arm rest.

Merle leaned back in his chair and laced his fingers behind his head.

I decided to just blurt it out. "You ever hear of

the *Garbage Man* killer, Cap'n?"

"I've heard the name," Merle answered. "Serial killer. Killed some college kids, I think. Back in the nineties. Why?"

I pointed at Lint to tell him he was up, and then waved the finger in Merle's direction. "Go ahead, tell him,"

Lint filled Merle in on everything he could remember about the case. After he was finished Merle said, "Let's keep the serial killer angle out of the media for now. Someone will make the connection soon enough. Until then it's just a homicide."

"What about the parents?" Lint asked.

"We have an address?" Merle asked.

"Yes," I replied.

"You two have lead on this," Merle informed us. "Work the Garbage Man connection. Perkins and Gwen will back you up and work this morning's homicide. Get together everything you can dig up on these killings. Keep me posted."

Lint and I got up and left Merle's office. "You hunt up the old files on this so we can familiarize ourselves with the original case," I said to Lint. "I'm going to speak with Perkins and Gwen. We'll have them notify the parents."

"Then can we grab something to eat?" Lint begged. "I'm starving."

I wanted to tell him to suck it up until lunch time, but my stomach was growling like a wolverine "Sure.

Can't let that corporation of yours start a massive layoff."

Lint guffawed good-naturedly and clapped me on the back. He always seemed to be a good sport about his weight. I guess the slob had to be. People put up with enough of his daily bullshit, I guess grinning and bearing it was his way of giving back.

After Lint bounced over to records I dialed Perkins' cell phone number.

"Perkins here."

"Hey, it's Jake. Where are ya?"

"Still at the scene."

"I'm gonna run back over. We gotta talk."

"Um ... I, uh," Perkins stammered. "We were ... um ... just getting ready to head back to the station. Can you wait there for us?"

"Sure I, guess." *What's up with him?* I wondered. I stood at my desk and looked around the squad room. It wasn't often I was the only one in the room. The only sound was the low volume of an old nineteen-inch color television that sat on a shelf across the room, above three gray, four-foot tall file cabinets. It was tuned to the news, and I wondered how long it would be until one of the anchors said, "This just in: Serial killer returns to North Myrtle Beach."

Next to the file cabinets sat a small wooden table with a coffee maker in dire need of cleaning, like always, some Styrofoam cups, and everything else needed to prepare that perfect cup of morning Joe. I walked over and poured myself a cup and stood sipping it while I watched the TV screen. Not so much the perfect cup of coffee.

I heard the door open and turned around. Dill Perkins came through the door first and went to his desk. He stowed his revolver in his desk drawer, and then turned to me, his face twisted in a scowl. "What?" he said. His tone was defensive.

"Nothing."

"You were staring at me."

"No I wasn't."

We both turned when the door opened again. It was Detective Gwen Lawrence. Without realizing it, I looked her up and down. There was something going on, I just couldn't put my finger on it.

"What?"

"Nothing."

"What are you looking at?"

"I just heard the door open, so I looked over."

She walked to her desk. She and Perkins never made eye contact. Then it dawned on me: She was wearing different clothes from when we were at Krispy Kreme. I glanced up at the clock. Sometime in the last hour, Gwen had gone home and changed her clothes. Why? Instinctively, my eyes went back to Perkins. He was wearing the same thing—he hadn't changed his clothes.

"Can I speak to you two out in the parking lot?" I asked.

They looked at each other nervously. "Uh, sure,

Jake," Perkins said.

I walked out first and they both followed.

"What's up?" Gwen asked.

I turned and leaned up against an unmarked cruiser. I folded my arms in front of me. "Merle told Lint and me to take the lead on this homicide. Lint and I think there could be a connection between this murder and a group of killings back in ninety-five. He's gathering up the files on *that* case now."

"Ninety-five? What's the connection?" Gwen asked.

"Just a few similarities Lint spotted. First thing I need you guys to do is head over to the girl's parents' house and inform them of her death. Bring them down to the morgue for a positive ID. The connection between the cold case and this one is to be kept between the four of us, and Merle, No one else. Got it?"

"Got it," Gwen said.

"That's it?" Perkins asked.

Gwen shot him a look.

"For now," I said.

"Okay," said Perkins. He turned and went back inside. Gwen followed him.

Lint stood next to his desk holding a cardboard box. Gwen and Perkins returned to their desks, retrieved their firearms and walked back past me without saying a word.

I turned and watched them walk through the door and then looked back toward Lint.

"I wonder how long those two have been screwing," Lint observed casually.

Chapter Four

We decided to order take-out from the Plantation Pancake House. I told Lint that if he went and picked it up, I would pay. He quickly agreed.

I brought the two boxes containing the files Lint had retrieved into the lounge and began spreading the different folders on the coffee table. The files were color-coded; each victim was represented by a different color sticker on the front of each file. The files pertaining to Mary McNeill were marked with green stickers. One file in each color group contained a photo of the victim Scotch taped to the front.

I made four neat piles, one for each victim: Mary McNeill, Sharon Jackson, Monica Thomas, and Betty Lloyd. I stared at each photograph for a second, wondering where to begin.

Mary McNeill had shoulder-length blonde hair, a tiny mole under left eye, and a set of chompers rivaled only by the Osmond family.

Sharon Jackson had long black hair. There was no telling exactly how long—it spilled far beyond the bottom border of the three by five photograph.

Monica Thomas was African American. Her dark hair was cut close to the scalp like the old "speedballs" most of us got every summer as kids.

Betty Lloyd was a brunette, a brunette with big blue eyes and a cute little freckle-covered nose that crinkled when she smiled.

The pictures showed no obvious connection between these young women. They had different hair colors, different facial features, even different ethnic backgrounds. The killer didn't seem to have a type as far as looks went.

I chose to start with Sharon Jackson's file first, for no other reason, I suppose, than I once dated a girl named Sharon. I opened her folder. Sharon Jackson was twenty years old in 1995. She came from a small town in Montana called Winnett, population less that two hundred. There was one less person the day Sharon left Big Sky Country for the Palmetto State to attend Coastal Carolina University, where she was murdered during her sophomore year.

A maintenance man found Sharon in a dumpster behind a McDonald's on a Sunday morning in October. The maintenance guy didn't know it at the time, but she was the second victim of the Garbage Man killer. He wasn't called the Garbage Man killer at that point. The local FOX TV affiliate, WFXB, didn't coin that phrase until two days later.

The lead detective on the case was Ray McPherson. I had read through most of his notes on Ms. Jackson by the time Lint returned with our breakfast. He sat one of the two Styrofoam to-go containers on the coffee table in front of me. "Here ya go," he said. "I couldn't remember if you said bacon or sausage."

"Sausage," I replied.

"I got you bacon."

"Of course you did." I opened the lid, picked up the plastic fork and dug into my scrambled eggs. My first bite of pork nirvana told me that I was glad he went with bacon, but I didn't let on.

When Lint tried to cut into his big stack of pancakes—which he liberally slathered with syrup—with the side of his plastic fork, it snapped in half. "Crap!"

"Just use your fingers," I joked.

"I'm not an animal!" he shot back angrily.

"Could have fooled me," I commented under my breath.

"What?"

"Nothing."

Lint picked up one of the pancakes with his fingertips and bit into it. He laid it back in the container and licked his fingers, sounding eerily like Hannibal Lecter chowing down on somebody's liver. Not a noise I wanted to hear while eating my own breakfast. Lint left the room and returned with one of the spoons that sat in a cup next to the coffee maker.

"Where should I start?" Lint asked, looking down at the folders.

I handed him the Sharon Jackson folder and said, "Why don't I read a file and then you look it over after me. Maybe you'll catch something I didn't."

"Good thinking." Lint took the file in his fat syrupy fingers and I chose the Monica Thomas folder next. Ms. Thomas was the first victim. A freshman at Coastal Carolina, studying communication, she was failing most of her classes. The lead investigator on the case, Detective McPherson, wrote in his notes that Monica's friends said she spent more time sleeping late and going to the beach than she did in class. That was understandable to me, because Bree and I spent a lot of time at the beach when we first moved down here, as well. No one could resist the pull of the ocean, and college kids were especially susceptible to its spell.

"Did you know this McPherson?" I asked.

"Sure … I guess … not really. He was here for the first few years that I was here, but he was a detective and I was in a uniform for that whole time. He retired shortly after all this insanity. He got in his twenty and he was gone."

"He still live around here?"

"I'm not sure. Don't think I've seen him since his retirement party."

"Let's get a current address on him. It would be nice to pick his brain."

"If he has any brain cells left."

"What do you mean?"

"Big drinker. Rumor was, retirement may not have been *his* choice, if ya know what I mean."

"I'd like to talk to him just the same."

Lint crammed the last bite of his pancakes into his mouth and said, "I'll see what I can find."

I returned to the Monica Thomas file. When I was finished with that, I grabbed the Mary McNeill folder. Mary was by far the prettiest of the victims; she was also the youngest, only seventeen. She wouldn't have been eighteen until December. She was a local girl, just like this morning's victim. She had graduated from North Myrtle Beach High School the summer before and still lived at home with her family. She was studying law and government. She wanted to be a police officer.

When I came to the end of Mary's file I thought I had missed something. There were no post-mortem photographs, no notes on where the body was found. I went back through the pages. I hadn't missed anything. Mary McNeill's body was never found.

Lint walked back through the door and I looked up from the paperwork. "Mary McNeill, the third victim. Her body was never recovered."

"Huh, I didn't remember that."

Lint shook his head thoughtfully. His multi-chins swayed like a fleshy chandelier. I hid my disgust and asked,

"What did you find on McPherson?"

"He has *no* more brain cells … he's dead."

"When?"

"Ninety-eight."

"Not much of a retirement."

"Eighteen months, to be exact."

"What got him?"

"Heart attack."

"Wife remarry?"

"Have no idea."

"Let's pay her a visit," I said, and then picked up the Betty Lloyd file.

"Better yet, you want me to get a hold of her and have her come in?" Lint asked.

"Sure."

Betty Lloyd was also a local girl, but that's the only thing she had in common with Mary McNeill. I didn't have a lot of experience with serial homicides—most cops don't—but it didn't take a genius to see that the victimology in this case was all over the place.

You wouldn't know it from the photograph, but Ms. Lloyd was a few years older than the other girls. She was twenty-eight. She wasn't a college student, never had been as far as I could tell from her file. She lived with her mother in a trailer on Mallard Street and worked as a waitress at the Hard Rock Café in Myrtle Beach. When I made it to the end of Betty Lloyd's file I noticed there was also something different about *her*. She showed no signs of sexual assault.

I tossed the folder back on to the coffee table. "One unknown subject, four victims, with no clear victimology. First and second follow the same MO. No body found with the third. The fourth victim and today's victim follow the same MO, but different from the first two."

"Makes it kind of difficult to come up with a profile on the killer," Lint commented.

"No shit. The only thing McPherson's profile says was that the subject was a male."

"Well, that narrows it down."

"I'm trying to figure out what made McPherson think the third victim was even connected. With no body, why wasn't Mary McNeill listed as a missing person?"

Lint shrugged. "It would have been nice to pick his brain."

"Doesn't look like he had a partner on this," I pointed out. "I wonder why?"

"Smaller force back then. I think there were only two detectives at the time. *I* was still in a uniform."

"Who was the other detective?"

Lint thought for a second. "I don't remember."

"Let's find out. Maybe we'll pay him a visit, too."

As Lint and I exited the lounge, the colorful, fast-moving graphics on the television caught my eye. In the upper left-hand corner of the screen the graphics chyron said LIVE. The bottom chyron read SERIAL KILLER RESURFACES IN NORTH MYRTLE BEACH.

"Son of a bitch!" I shouted.

Lint went quickly to the TV and turned up the volume. A blown-dry anchorman beamed at the camera.

Once again, thank you for joining us this morning for this WMBF special report. WMBF has just learned from our sources of a possible resurfacing of a serial killer who murdered several young women in the fall of 1995.

The body of a young woman, whose identity is being withheld until the notification of family members, was discovered this morning at the Krispy Kreme donut shop on North Kings Highway.

Lint and I stood motionless watching the broadcast.

The body was discovered by an assistant manager around seven o'clock this morning. We go live to Shelly Curry at the scene. Shelly, what do you have for us?

Merle's office door swung open. His face was fire engine red. "Who the hell leaked it?" he shouted.

Lint and I both shook our heads and looked back at the screen.

Thanks, Hal. As you can see, this Krispy Kreme store, normally a favorite haunt of commuters and tourists is empty now while police conduct their investigation. Details are sketchy at this hour, as police are being tight lipped about their investigation. What we do know is that the body of a young woman was found early this morning in the dumpster you see behind me.

"Turn it off," I said, and then my phone rang. I grabbed it from its holder, clipped to my belt. "Stellar," I answered. It was Perkins. "I know. We're watching it now … I have no idea. Please tell me you had already spoken with the parents … Thank God … I need you to get me the name and address, if he's still alive, of the other detective on the job at the time of the first killings … hold on."

I glanced back up at the screen. A gentleman in his early seventies was speaking. The chyron identified him as Retired Detective Roger Grayson.

"Turn it up," I said. Lint shook his chins and turned it up for the second time.

And in your expert opinion, Detective Grayson, the plastic anchorman asked, *do you think the North Myrtle Beach Police Department will be able to stop this serial killer this time around?*

Grayson got a confused look on his face. *Well, we did everything we could in ninety-five. The killings just st—*

Detective Grayson, do you feel at all responsible for this latest murder?

Grayson looked off camera and mumbled something, then began yanking off his lapel mic. *This is bullshit. They said they wanted to ask m—.* His voice trailed off as he stalked away.

The camera jumped back to the news anchor. *We apologize to our viewers for these technical difficulties.*

Grayson must have still been in the studio because you could hear him from somewhere off camera hollering *blood-sucking pieces of shit!* I chuckled a little in agreement.

"Perkins, the detective's name is Roger Grayson," I informed him. "And he's very much alive. Get me his address and see if you can get him in here this afternoon around four."

Perkins said, "Will do," and hung up.

I turned to Lint. "Forget calling McPherson's wife. You got her address?"

"Yeah."

"Let's go pay her a visit."

"Without calling?"

"Yeah. Why? You think if she knew we were coming she'd bake a cake?"

"Wouldn't that be nice," Lint said.

Chapter Five

Jean MacPherson lived over in Windy Hill, on Pinecrest Street. The house sat back from the street about seventy-five feet, in a wooded area. It was a blue, two-story home with natural, wood-grained siding, a large, screened-in front porch, and a rustic staircase leading to the second floor. Nestled cozily amongst the pines, it looked more like a camp in the Adirondacks than a home in North Myrtle Beach, near the ocean.

I brought the unmarked cruiser to a stop in the gravel driveway and Lint and I got out. Just being in this fragrant woodsy setting made me want to take a deep breath, so I did.

Lint looked over the top of the car. "What was that for?"

"Just smelling the trees," I answered. "Makes me a little homesick."

Lint swung the passenger side door closed and walked toward the staircase. "Upstate New York, isn't it?"

"Bronx," I corrected. "But we would camp in the Adirondacks almost every year when I was a kid."

"Hey, my second wife lives in Old Forge," Lint said, in a tone that made it sound like we now had more in common.

Lint stepped aside to let me ascend the stairs first. I wondered if he did this because I was in charge or just in case there was a large dog.

I rapped on the door a couple times and then pressed the doorbell. The bell was loud enough to hear outside so I knew it worked. I waited a few seconds and knocked again. "Mrs. McPherson," I called out. I couldn't hear any movements or sound coming from inside. "Run back down and look in the garage. See if there's a car in there."

Lint turned and hurried down the stairs. I could see each step bow under his weight as he went.

I knocked again.

A few seconds later Lint poked his head around the corner of the house. "Two cars in the garage," he said.

I tried the doorknob; it was locked.

I heard a woman's voice call out. "Can I help you?"

I turned and started down the steps. A woman was walking toward us from a tidy yellow house that sat at the corner of Pinecrest and Windy Hill Road.

Lint and I met her at the end of the McPhersons' driveway. We both presented our badges.

"We're looking for Jean McPherson," I said.

"Is everything okay?" the woman asked. "I'm Irma Lambert." She glanced back toward the house on the corner. "I live right there."

"Yes, everything is fine," Lint responded. "We just needed to ask her a few questions."

"Her *husband* was a cop, but you probably already knew that," Irma said.

"Yes," I responded.

"Is this about that serial killer? It's been all over the television."

"Is everything okay?" we heard another woman call out.

The three of us looked to the house next door to the McPhersons. A stoop-shouldered, blue-haired old woman stood at the end of her driveway with the aid of her walker.

Irma Lambert waved to her. "Not sure, Kay. These gentlemen are cops. They're here about the serial killer."

"We're not here about the serial killer, ma'am," I informed her.

"Oh my goodness!" Kay shouted back, just as another man was walking through his yard toward us. "What's going on?" he shouted.

Kay yelled back. "They think the serial killer is in our neighborhood."

"Jesus Christ," Lint whispered.

I turned to him and whispered back. "Go talk to those two. Assure them there's no serial killer in their neighborhood. I'll handle Mrs. Lambert."

"On it."

I put up my hand. "Mrs. Lambert we're just here to ask Mrs. McPherson about an old case of her husband's. This has nothing to do with a serial killer."

Mrs. Lambert winked as though she was in on the "deception." She turned an imaginary key over her pinched-tight lips and said, "Mums the word!"

I went along with it and just said, "Thanks for your cooperation, ma'am. Do you know where we can find Mrs. McPherson?"

"She went to visit her daughter in Georgia. Supposed to be back day after tomorrow. I've been bringing in her mail. She travels quite a bit since the warden died."

I cocked my head. "The warden?"

"Oh, I probably shouldn't have said that. You and him might have been friends."

"Are you talking about Detective McPherson?" I asked. I glanced over toward Lint. He was following Kay and the other man up the driveway toward Kay's house. He turned and looked in my direction as he walked along, and then disappeared through the open garage door.

"Yeah," Irma answered. "Ray was kind of— pardon my French, young man—a bastard. Jean called him the warden. He ruled that home with an iron fist. Those two kids of theirs couldn't wait to get away from there. I always felt bad for Jean because the kids never came back to visit, and the warden always had some reason that she couldn't go visit them."

"But she visits them now?" I asked.

"Oh, yes. She goes out and sees them a few times a year. They even come home for visits now. The boy, Ray Jr., lives in Tennessee, I think."

"She never remarried?"

"Ha-ha! I asked her awhile back why she never remarried—ya know, she was only fifty-three when he kicked the bucket. She said, 'The only thing I ever hated in my whole life was being married. Why would I do it again?'"

I chuckled. "I guess you can't argue with that."

"No, you can't, Detective—what did you say your name was?"

"Stellar, Jake Stellar."

Her eyes shot to the sky in thought. "Wasn't that an old cop show?"

"No," I answered a little curtly, since I'd heard that line at least a thousand times. I thanked Irma Lambert for her help and then went to search for Lint.

"Lint!" I called out from the garage of Kay what's-her-name's house. "Lint!"

"In here!" he shouted back.

I walked through an open door that led to the kitchen. Lint, Kay, and the gentleman from across the street were seated at the kitchen table. Each of them had a cup of coffee in front of them as well as a piece of chocolate cake with white frosting. Lint was cramming a forkful into his mouth as I entered.

"Kay offered us cake," Lint informed me.

"I see that."

Lint motioned to the man seated on his right. "She asked me and Bart if we could move her couch to the other wall."

"I see."

"Would you like a slice of cake and a cup of coffee, Detective?" Kay asked.

I thought about saying no, but the look of sheer joy on Avis Lint's face told me I had to try a piece. *Oh, well,* I thought. *If you can't beat them, join them.* "Sure, that would be great."

Kay got up creakily from the table and guided her walker over to the counter. "Good, because I also need you to move a dresser for me."

Chapter Six

After I finished my piece of cake, and Lint finished his second, we jumped in the car and headed back to the station. While eating our cake and drinking our coffee Kay and Bart filled us in on the late night fighting and screaming matches that had gone on at the McPherson house back in the late eighties and most the nineties. Kay told us about the few times that the McPherson children, Elizabeth and Ray Jr., had spent the night at her house to get away from the fighting. Bart told us about the time he almost got in a fistfight with Ray McPherson over parking in the street. Seems Ray had backed into Bart's car and decided it was somehow Bart's fault.

Both Kay and Bart agreed that Jean McPherson was a saint, a wonderful woman who didn't deserve the shit her husband put her through.

They both spoke about never calling the police because Ray *was* a police officer and none of them wanted to be harassed by the police, so they minded their own business the best they could.

I didn't know Ray McPherson, and Lint said he didn't know him very well either, but I can't imagine dying and having my whole neighborhood be glad I was gone.

Kay had asked me if I wanted to take a second piece of cake home with me. She was sure my wife would enjoy a piece. She was probably right, but I passed.

Lint confessed to me on the way back to the station that the only reason he went in for a piece of cake was because he knew we could get the scoop on Ray and Jean. I confessed to him that he was a goddamn liar. He laughed, but didn't argue.

When we returned to the station, Perkins and Gwen were in the lounge reading over the files on the first four cases. Perkins sat on the couch, a Styrofoam cup of coffee on the end table next to him. He was reading the Mary McNeill file. Gwen was seated in a chair across from him. Her legs were crossed, and Sharon Jackson file lay balanced on her knee.

When we entered the lounge, Perkins pulled off his reading glasses and said, "They never found the McNeill's body."

"We know!" Lint and I chorused in perfect harmony.

"Couple of comedians," said Perkins, laughing in spite of himself. "Then why is it grouped in with these homicides?"

"That we don't know," I responded.

"Did you speak to McPherson's widow?" Gwen asked.

"She's out of town until Tuesday," I answered. "Did you speak with Roger Grayson?"

Perkins nodded. "We asked him if he could come in this afternoon and answer a few questions."

"And?" Lint asked.

"*And*," Gwen replied, "he said he was already made to look like a fool once today by those—"—She made finger quotes—"—*blood sucking bastards on the news*, and he wasn't about to drive back here and let it happen again. But if we would like, we can drive out to *his* place and ask all the questions we want."

"What's the address?" Lint asked.

Perkins grabbed his note pad off the coffee table. "213 Geralds Avenue … in Mullins."

Lint rolled his eyes. "Dammit! That's an hour away."

"How did the TV station get him there so fast?" I asked.

"He said they had a driver en route before they even got a hold of him," Perkins answered.

"Real go-getters," I commented.

"Literally," Gwen pointed out.

"We better get started for Grayson's place," I said. "I want you two to head out to the college. I know its Sunday, but I want a list of her professors and a list of her friends. I want to know where she was last night. I want to know who she was with. I want to know who the last person was to see her alive. Pull her phone records. I want to know everyone she spoke with in the last two weeks. Find out if she has a boyfriend."

Perkins was hastily scribbling in his pad as I spoke. When he finished he looked up. "Anything else, master?"

I grinned. "That should keep you busy."

I turned and started for the door.

"Oh, and Grayson said one more thing," Perkins called out.

I turned back. "What's that?"

"He said we could expect a visitor pretty soon."

Just as I asked who, Perkins' eyes shot past me, through the window, and into the squad room. I turned. There was a gentleman standing there. He gazed around the room and then our eyes met. The guy was about five-eleven, with short gray hair. His face was clean-shaven. He wore faded jeans, a navy-blue T-shirt with the Polo logo on the left breast, and a gray checkered cardigan. In his right hand was a file folder.

I walked out into the squad room and asked, "Can I help you?" the man didn't show much emotion. He didn't speak right away, continuing to survey the room as though he was searching for something different, something out of place. Finally he snapped out of it and approached me with his hand extended.

"Sorry, sir" he said. "I haven't been here in a

while, eight years to be exact."

We shook hands. "Is there something I can do for you?"

"My name is Archie McNeill. My friends call me Mac. I'm Mary McNeill's father."

I turned and looked behind me to see Lint, Gwen, and Perkins, all standing in the doorway. I then returned my focus to McNeill. "Detective Jake Stellar. I think I can guess why you're here."

"Right. I saw on the news about the serial killer" he handed me the folder he was carrying. "These are some notes, and files I've collected over the years. I thought maybe they could be of some help to you, if the case is reopened. Are you the lead investigator?"

I didn't answer him as I glanced inside the folder. "We appreciate your help, Mr. McNeill." My tone was noncommittal. I didn't want to get his hopes up.

"They never found her. I thought if you were reopening the case, then maybe I could get her back."

I flipped through the pages in the file folder. There were pictures of Mary. Many of the files appeared to be ones I had already read. I didn't know what to tell him so I said, "Thank you, we'll read through these. Every little bit might help." I closed the folder.

"Do you have any leads?" he asked.

"We're looking into a few things," I answered.

"Any suspects?"

"Mr. McNeill—."

"Please, call me Mac."

I knew what he was doing. He wanted me to call him Mac. His friends called him Mac. He wanted to think of me as a friend, and vice versa. He thought if we were friends I would care about him and his daughter; that somehow, maybe it would make me try harder. "Mac," I explained, as I looked into his sad eyes. "I promise you we are doing everything we can at this point."

Mac ran his fingers through his hair and scratched the back of his head. "Detective McPherson promised me the same thing twenty years ago. Then the abductions stopped, he retired, he died, and the case went cold."

"I'm not McPherson," I told him. "I can only imagine the pain you've felt every day for all these years, and I know that when you heard we were reopening the case you felt some hope again. Hold on to that hope, Mac. Go home. Let us do our job." I waved Lint over. "Detective Lint will get your contact information—we'll have a few questions to ask you—and then walk you to your car."

I thanked him again and reached out to shake. He grabbed my hand and held on tight. "Jake, do you know what the last thing I said to her that morning was?"

My voice cracked when I answered, "No."

"I told her I loved her. I told her, 'Be careful, you're the most important thing I own.' Just as always she laughed and said, 'I know, Daddy. I love you, too.'"

Chapter Seven

Against my better judgment, I had Lint drive the hour to Mullins. I had placed a call to Grayson and he was expecting us.

As I rode along in the passenger seat, I read the file Archie McNeill had given me. Just as I had thought when I first glanced at it, it was mostly a rehash of the file I already had on his daughter. What it didn't tell me was why Ray McPherson felt Mary McNeill was part of this case. I hoped Roger Grayson could shed some light on that.

You're the most important thing I own. Those words were stuck in my head like a bad song. The line was a running gag between a father and a daughter he loved more than life itself. As I read through Archie's notes it became more and more obvious exactly how true that was.

Within two years of Mary's disappearance,

Archie and his wife, Tamara, had split up; a year later they divorced. Mac lost his job at the lumber store where he had worked for fifteen years. In '99 a friend of Tamara's suggested grief counseling; she went once a week for about a year. In October 2000 Tamara called Archie and asked him to come over to the house. When he arrived, the door was open. Archie called out for Tamara and searched through the house. He found her hanging from a truss in the garage. A small wooden stool lay on its side at her feet.

Archie was right, Mary *was* the most important thing in their lives, and when she disappeared it all fell apart. He was also right about another thing: shaking hands, calling each other by first names, and staring into each other's eyes as he told me the final words he uttered to his daughter did make me care a lot more.

As we drove along West Dogwood Drive, I glanced down at the map I had brought up on my phone. "Take a right up here on Seaboard Avenue, and then Liberty Street is the second left." I exited out of the Google map app. "Handy little app," I commented as I returned my cell to its holder.

Lint slowed and turned onto Liberty. I looked at the first mailbox we came to. "Here it is on the right."

Lint pulled to the side of the street and turned off the engine. Liberty Street had no sidewalks or curbs, and everyone's driveway was two dirt tire tracks down the side of their house. Grayson's house looked almost exactly like the other three houses on his street: one story, white vinyl siding, and a front porch constructed from cement blocks. Five four-by-fours held up the porch roof, and between each post was a wooden railing with square spindles. Two green, plastic deck chairs sat on the porch, and in the corner were three or four fishing poles leaning against the house.

I reached into the back seat and grabbed the files I had brought, and we got out of the car. We started up the makeshift pathway that had been made by dropping chunks of cement here and there in the yard, from the street to the front steps.

Grayson's front door opened and he stepped out onto the porch as we reached the bottom of the steps. He looked every second of his seventy-five years. "Good afternoon," I said. "Roger Grayson?"

He stuck his hands in his pockets, arched his back, and rose up on the balls of his bare feet. "That's me," he grumbled. His old faded jeans had a large hole in the knee, and the sleeves of his long-sleeved flannel shirt were rolled up past is elbows. His tongue moved around the toothpick sticking out of the corner of his mouth.

I stuck out my hand. "Detective Jake Stellar—we spoke on the phone. This is Detective Avis Lint."

Grayson looked us up and down. His hands didn't leave his pockets. "Jake Stellar. Ain't that one of them detectives on that old TV show?"

"Not that I'm aware of, sir," I responded. I heard Lint snicker behind me.

Grayson looked over my shoulder. "What the fuck are you laughing about, tubby? Your family named you after the shit a dryer leaves behind."

The smile left Lint's face.

"Um, can we step inside, Mr. Grayson?" I asked.

"The name's Roger." He turned and walked back through his front door and we followed.

As we walked through the living room to the dining room, the sickly sweet smell of marijuana was overwhelming. I glanced down at the water bong sitting on the coffee table. Next to it was a pot leaf-decorated Bic lighter and an ashtray containing two or three roaches. "It's for medicinal purposes," Grayson informed us. I had strong doubts about that, but busting the old stoner wasn't what we were there for.

"What's the matter with you, Mr.—er—Roger?" Lint asked.

"None of your fucking business, lard-ass" Grayson shot back. He sat down in one of the four chairs that surrounded the dining room table. "So, what can I do for you gentlemen?" With his foot he shoved one of the chairs away from the table. "Have a seat."

We sat and I placed the folders on the table. I slid Mary McNeill's file in front of Grayson. "Would you have any idea why Detective McPherson thought Ms. McNeill was abducted by the same man who murdered the other three? Her body was never found."

Grayson stared at the photograph of Mary McNeill as I spoke, and then opened the folder. "I didn't work this case, you know," he explained as he shuffled through the pages. "There were only two of us detectives back then. The chief had Ray working on this round the clock, and I was working on everything else."

"He never spoke to you about a subject profile, or any leads?" Lint asked.

"Oh, sure, he bounced ideas and thoughts off me, but—"

"But what?" I asked.

"This couldn't have come at a worse time for him."

I crossed my forearms on the table and leaned forward. "What do you mean?"

"Ray and his wife ... they fought a lot. Ya know?"

I nodded. "We spoke to some neighbors of theirs who told us the same thing. Did he ever confide in you? Did he ever mention why they fought so much?"

"He didn't have to confide in me, everybody knew why they fought. It was his drinking and whore chasing. He was always banging some broad on the side. He was never careful, he didn't care if Jean found out or not."

"Sounds like a great guy," Lint said.

Grayson pointed a finger. "You watch your fuckin' mouth, tubby. McPherson was a good cop."

"Sorry," Lint said.

"How many times you been married, tubby?"

"Four."

"Married now?"

"No."

"Probably 'cause you ain't no goddamn angel

either." He looked at me. "You?"

"Just once, and still married. Almost twenty years."

"Congadu-fuckin-lations!" Grayson hollered. He picked up one of the pages in the file. "Oh, yeah ... I remember this guy, the girl's father, Artie, Archie, or something."

"Archie," I said.

"Yeah. Poor bastard. She was an only child, his girl. Felt bad for that guy. He was always coming into the station. Every time he heard about a young girl being killed or raped, he was right back down there. Used to carry around his own files. Heard he spent some time in the nut house over in Columbia."

"He showed up at the station this morning," I said.

Grayson shook his head as he laid down the paper. "Poor bastard. Always thought he was gonna find her alive someday. Always had hope. Poor bastard." Grayson gazed over my shoulder in thought for a second. "Don't know why Ray thought she was connected to the others. I need a drink. You guys thirsty?"

"No, thanks," I said. Lint was too cowed by Roger's taunts to say yea or nay.

Roger got up and pulled a rocks glass from a row of cabinets that hung from the ceiling and separated the kitchen from the dining room. He sat the glass on the countertop underneath the cabinets. He grabbed a bottle of Evan William's bourbon from another cupboard and poured the glass half full. By the time he sat back down it was almost gone.

"Do you know if McPherson kept personal files on cases he worked?" I asked.

"I would imagine so," he answered. "We all keep those damn files on unsolved cases. *You* must."

I nodded. "I do."

Grayson threw a thumb over his shoulder. "Got drunker than hell one night about ten years back. Took every bit of paperwork and files I had laying around here and built a bon fire right out there in the yard. Thought it would stop me from agonizin' about the fuckers that got away."

"Did it?" Lint asked.

"Nope, but the ganja does."

I had Grayson read through the other files in hopes that it might jog something loose in his old drug and alcohol addled brain, but it didn't. The only things we left his house knowing were that Ray McPherson screwed around a lot, Archie McNeill may have spent some time in a mental institution, and that seventy-year-old, arthritic fingers could still roll a joint pretty damn fast.

When we climbed back into the car, Lint said, "Well, that was a wasted three hours." He made a U-turn and swung a right back on to Seaboard Avenue. "There's a Burger King on McIntyre Street."

"How the hell do you know that?" I asked.

"I've driven through here a few times. You want to get something to eat?"

"Sure, tubby."

Chapter Eight

It was almost five o'clock by the time we got back to North Myrtle Beach. I had called Bree to tell her I would be late. Meanwhile Perkins had called me to say that the medical examiner's report on Paige Samuels' autopsy was finished and on my desk.

Gwen was at her desk and Perkins was at his when Lint and I walked through the door.

Perkins pointed at my cluttered desk. "It's right on top," he said, referring to the ME's report.

"You speak with the parents?" I asked.

Perkins leaned back in his chair. "Yes. Paige does have a boyfriend." He glanced down at his notes. "Mark Olsen, twenty-four. He's been at his parent's house in Bishopville all weekend. His father said he got there around four-thirty Friday afternoon and he's still there. He doesn't have any classes on Mondays so he's not back in town until tomorrow evening."

"Had they already been notified of Paige's death?"

"Yes. The Samuelses notified Mark and his parents about an hour before I called."

"How did you make out at the college?"

"There's a list of her teachers, classes, and the names of close friends that her parents gave me. The list is under the ME's report."

I moved the report aside and picked up the list of her friends. "Was she with any of these people last night?"

"Yes," Perkins answered. "The third name down, Noreen Hass. Noreen and Paige grew up together. The Hass's live one street over from the Samuelses, on Swan Lake Drive."

"You speak to Noreen?"

"Yes," Gwen responded. "Noreen said Paige picked her up last night around nine-thirty.

They went to the Malibu's Surf Bar first and stayed there until around midnight. After Malibu's they came back to North Myrtle Beach and stopped at Molly Darcy's—Noreen works as a bartender there. They sat at the bar and had drinks until around one-thirty. They left, and Paige dropped Noreen off at her home. As far as *she* knew, Paige was going straight home."

Lint spoke for me, too, when he wondered aloud, "What could have happened in the one block that they live from each other?"

"You took the words right out of my mouth, Lint," I agreed.

"And where is Paige's car?" Perkins threw in.

"Her cell phone is also missing," Gwen said.

"Why don't you two call it a day," I said.

"Are you sure?" Perkins asked.

"Yeah, go ahead. You and Gwen can talk to her teachers tomorrow, as well as the rest of the names on this list. Lint and I will hunt up Betty Lloyd's mother tomorrow and see if we can speak with *her*."

Perkins got up from his desk and stretched luxuriously. "Sounds good to me."

Gwen agreed and got up from her desk too, and they both headed toward the door.

As I looked over the ME's findings I remembered something and called out to Perkins. "Hey! What did you get on the security cameras at the scene?"

The one on the back of the building is broken, hasn't worked in a few weeks. The one on the side of the building doesn't show the dumpster. You can see the side parking lot and part of Thirteenth Avenue South. There was no traffic on thirteenth anywhere near the time she was dumped, so whoever put her there came by way of Outrigger Road."

"Tomorrow, check with the other businesses along there that have their backs to Outrigger Road," I suggested. "See if they have any cameras that might have caught something."

"You got it, boss," Perkins said.

"You guys doing anything tonight?" Lint asked.

Gwen and Perkins looked at each other and then at Lint. "No," they said in unison.

"Either one of you want to have a drink later, or grab something to eat?"

Perkins said, "I was planning on turning in early tonight."

"I'm having dinner at my parents' house," Gwen said.

"Oh, okay," Lint said. "Maybe another time."

"Yeah, sure … another time," said Perkins. They both turned and walked out.

I turned to Lint and asked, "Since when did you ever want to spend your evenings with either one of those two?"

"I didn't, but did you notice how they both said they had nothing to do, but when I asked they both suddenly had an excuse?"

"Maybe they just didn't want to have a drink with *you*."

"Or maybe they're sleeping together and their real plan is to meet up later."

"I doubt they're sleeping together, and maybe you should mind your own business."

"Whatever. You need me to do anything else?"

"No, you might as well head on home too."

"You got it, boss."

"Don't call me boss."

"Perkins called you boss."

"Bye," I said.

After Lint left I took advantage of the peace and quiet of the empty squad room. I read the autopsy report. The bloodwork wouldn't be back until tomorrow afternoon. According to the report Paige Samuels had been murdered somewhere else and then transported to the dumpsite. Estimated time of death was between one-thirty and three-thirty; I already knew that. I also already knew that the cause of death was blunt force trauma to the back of the skull, probably with a metal object. Unlike the other girls, Paige's left leg was fractured, as well as her left forearm. The palms of her hands were scraped up and the medical examiner had removed bits of asphalt from the scrapes. Ms. Samuels's eyes had been glued open, but she had not been sexually assaulted. This was puzzling, because the whole purpose of gluing the eyes open was so they had to watch their attacker during the assault. Was the subject interrupted before the assault? Was he not able to perform—after all, the Garbage Man killer would be twenty years older now.

Merle's office door opened and he walked into the squad room. "Still here?"

"Yeah. Just going over the autopsy report. I'm gonna read through the old reports again. Probably head home after that."

"Any strong leads?"

"Not yet."

"Well, good luck. See ya tomorrow," Merle said, rolling up the sleeves of his white, button-down dress shirt. As he walked by me I caught the competing odors of Brute aftershave and stale sweat. When he got to the door he turned around and said, "Hey, you think there's anything going on between Perkins and Gwen?"

"Do *you* think there is?"

"I don't know. They seemed to go out of their way today to not speak or look at each other. They just acted … funny."

"You want me to ask?"

"No, not yet. Just keep an eye on them."

"You got it, Cap'n."

Chapter Nine

It was after seven by the time I pulled my truck into the garage. I felt as though I had never brought this much work home with me before. My head was spinning with faces, names, places, and dates that I knew were somehow connected. But, how could they be connected when nothing seemed to fit together? It was like someone had dumped three jigsaw puzzles into the same box and said, "Here, put this together."

I sat in my truck for a few seconds with my hands on the steering wheel, staring straight ahead. How were Mary McNeill and Betty Lloyd connected? Other than both being women, there were no similarities. There was one piece missing from my box of assorted puzzle pieces, and that piece was Detective Ray McPherson. I couldn't help feeling that if he were still alive, I could get the answers I needed to solve this case. I hoped Jean McPherson might know something that would help. Maybe Ray mentioned something to her one night after work. Maybe she had information she didn't even know she had.

Sitting there in the truck like that, in the quiet, I had that thought that sometimes sneaks into my brain when I'm alone and stressed. Maybe I could have just one drink. Maybe I could handle it now. After all it's been eight years since my last drink. If I had a beer instead of the Scotch, would that really be falling off the wagon? I didn't have a problem with beer. Yeah, right. Famous last words.

I knew every thought I was having about the booze was just my own mind applying the peer pressure it thought it would take to get me off the wagon. Maybe someday I would fall for it, but today wasn't the day.

I figured by now Bree was probably wondering why I hadn't come into the house, so I got out of the truck and went in.

The first thing I noticed was the pink leash that was hanging from the hook where I usually hung my car keys. Then I looked down at the small bag of dog food that was sitting on the floor, propped up against the cupboards. *Oh crap, what has she done now?*

I walked through the kitchen and in to the living room. Bree was sitting on the floor, and what appeared to be a *very* small animal—part rat, part bat, and part dog—played with a larger, yellow, stuffed animal.

Bree looked up at me and smiled. "What do you think?"

"I think you've lost your mind."

"Isn't she adorable?"

"She's ... something."

"Look how small she is."

"I'm looking."

"She's a miniature Yorkie."

"How much?"

Bree swatted the stuffed animal across the room and the rat-thing chased it. Bree laughed gleefully. "Oh, my God, I can't believe how cute she is!"

I wondered if it was too late to make a trip to the liquor store. I watched as the rat-thing leapt into the air and came down on the stuffed duck. I almost grinned, but caught myself. "How much did you say it cost?"

"Guess what I named her?" Bree asked.

"Cujo."

"Nope."

"Ben? Willard?"

"No, really, guess."

"There's a million dog names in the world. How would I possibly guess?"

"Woofie."

"Woofie?"

Every time the dog would reach the stuffed duck it would try to stop but slide past it on the ceramic tile, and every time Bree would bust a gut. The little rat of a dog was cuter than shit, but I was not about to let on. "Did you eat?" I asked.

"Yes," Bree said, without looking up.

I waited to hear *what* she ate. Where were the leftovers for me? Watching Bree play with her new dog, I quickly realized that I would have to find the answers to these questions on my own.

I stepped back into the kitchen and went directly to the stove. There were no dirty pans. I glanced over at the sink. There were no dirty dishes. I went to the refrigerator. There were no food-filled plates covered in plastic wrap. Either she ate everything she made and cleaned the kitchen, or there was a fast food bag in the garbage. I went to the garbage can and stepped on the pedal, raising the lid, and peered inside. There it was, a crumpled-up Sonic bag. I am one hell of a detective. I could have looked inside the bag for the receipt to see what time she ate, but I figured I would just ask.

When I returned to the living room the same game of Throw the Duck was still in progress. "You had Sonic?" I asked.

"Great job, Sherlock. In what school did you learn your deductive skills?"

"Elementary," I shot back. There's nothing better than a wife who sets you up for the perfect delivery.

"You hungry?"

"Starving."

"Why don't you jump in the shower and I'll order a pizza?"

"Sounds like a plan," I informed her, and then bent over to kiss her.

*****

After my shower I put on a T-shirt and swimming trunks. It had warmed up nicely so we sat at the wrought iron patio set next to the pool eating our pizza. Bree drank water mixed with fruit from a plastic sports bottle. I was having ginger ale in a short glass over ice.

"What do ya got in that thing now?" I asked, noticing a fruit I hadn't seen in the bottle before.

Bree held it up. "Chunks of watermelon. It's good. You want to try it?"

"No."

"It's good for you. Watermelon has vitamin A, vitamin C, and it's loaded with lycopene and amino acids."

"Dr. Oz tell you that?"

"No, I read it on the Internet."

"What web site?"

Bree took a bite of her pizza. "None of your business."

"Was it the Dr. Oz web page?"

"No, it was the why-don't-you-shut-up web page. Now drop it."

"That's what I thought."

Woofie played under the table, first pouncing on Bree's feet and then mine. I removed a piece of pepperoni from my slice and tore it in half.

"What are you doing?" Bree asked.

"I was going to give the dog a piece of pepperoni."

Bree was incredulous. "You silly goose! You can't give a puppy like that pepperoni. It would make her sick."

I tossed it into my own mouth. "Sorry, dog, you would have loved it."

"Come here, Woofie." Bree picked up her new best friend and placed her on her lap. "Don't eat anything Daddy gives you."

Daddy? Good God, I've become the father of a little rat-dog.

"So, how was your day?" Bree *finally* asked.

"Long, and confusing."

"You want to talk about it?"

I did want to talk about it, but I didn't want to go into detail about it. I knew Bree had probably seen the story on the news, but seeing it on the news is a lot different than hearing it from me. The news is television and everyone knows it. Sure, it's a horrible story; young girls found dead in a dumpster, and the resurgence of a serial killer. But it's *still* television. When the story comes from me it becomes more real, more harsh, more horrible. "How much did you see on the news?" I asked.

Bree was petting the dog as she spoke. "They said a serial killer and rapist from the nineties may have resurfaced. They said a young college student was found this morning, dead, in a dumpster, behind the Krispy Kreme."

I sipped my ginger ale. "That's about it."

"What makes you think this morning's victim is connected to the four girls from the original case?"

"Condition of the body, where it was found, her age."

"What's the confusing part?"

"The first two victims were sexually assaulted, the fourth victim and this morning's victim weren't."

"Then how do you know it was the same guy?"

"Something he did to the bodies. Something that was never released to the press."

I could tell Bree wanted to ask what that something was but she restrained herself, asking instead, "What about the third girl?"

"Her body was never recovered."

"What's her connection to the other three?"

I sighed the sigh to end all sighs. "That's the confusing part. We don't know what the connection is."

"Can't you ask the detective who worked the case?"

"He died a long time ago, and there's nothing in the girls' file that sheds any light. His widow is alive. She's out of town right now. I'll speak with her the day after tomorrow."

"You think she might know something?"

"Who knows? Maybe he mentioned something about the case to her. Maybe he kept some personal files at home. If he did and we can get a look at them maybe it will tell us something."

"Maybe," Bree agreed. "But if someone came to our house and asked me something about a case you worked twenty years ago, I wouldn't be able to tell them anything."

Bree was right; I tried not to bring my work home with me very often. Being a nurse, she saw enough shit in the emergency room. I never felt like I should pile the shit I had seen on top of that. Maybe Ray McPherson was different. He didn't seem to mind yelling and fighting with his wife. Being faithful wasn't too important to him. So just maybe coming home from work at the end of the day, and telling his wife about the dead bodies of young women who had been raped and thrown in a dumpster was no big deal.

I shoved the crust of my third piece of pizza into my mouth and got up from the table. "You think that rat can swim?" I asked. I removed my shirt and laid it over the back of the chair.

"No!" Bree shot back. "She's only ten weeks old."

"I think they're born knowing how to swim."

"I don't think they are."

I walked over to the deep end of the pool and

jumped in feet first. I sank to the bottom and stayed below the surface as long as I could hold my breath. *I'm sure that dog can swim*, I thought as I slowly floated upward. When I reached the surface I filled my lungs with air and leaned backwards, floating on my back.

While I was under, Bree had walked to the steps and sat down, putting her feet in the water. The dog was lying next to her. I rolled over and did the breast stroke toward her. "How much did you say that thing cost?" I asked for the third time.

"I didn't," she responded.

"How much?"

"How much do you think she was?"

"Two hundred?"

Bree pointed her index finger in the air.

"Five hundred?"

She kept pointing upward. I swam to her and put my chin on her knee. She leaned forward and kissed me on the forehead. "Fifteen hundred," she said.

I closed my eyes tightly. "Fifteen hundred dollars," I repeated.

"Is that too much?" she asked with a big grin. She picked up the dog and held it face to face with me. "Give Daddy kisses."

"Do *not* give Daddy kisses," I protested.

Bree laughed out loud. "She's worth fifteen hundred dollars."

"We'll see."

Bree turned the dog around and gave it a peck on the nose. "Daddy said, 'We'll see,' Woofie."

I pushed away from Bree. *Three hundred and seventy-five dollars a pound*, I thought, as I floated across the water. *I better be getting sex tonight.*

Chapter Ten

Bree was up the next morning and out the door before six. If I had been up by five I could have had scrambled eggs with bell pepper and tomato, and toast with slices of avocado. I got up at six-thirty, and the unfrosted blueberry Pop-Tarts were just fine.

I walked out to the driveway and grabbed the Monday morning edition of the Sun News and read it at the dining room table with my second cup of coffee—flavored with pumpkin spice because, after all, it was October.

As I sat there a high-pitched yelp came from the living room. *Oh yeah,* I thought, *the dog.* I got up from the table and went into the living room. The rat-dog was standing in her crate staring at me, her one inch tail wagging feverishly. "What's the matter, dog, don't like being in that cage?" She yelped again so I let him out. "You hungry?"

I walked back into the dining room and the million-dollar dog followed me. I broke off a tiny piece of my Pop-Tart and held it out; she ate it from the palm of my hand. "Good, isn't it?" I gave her another piece. "Keep your mouth shut about this Pop-Tart. We'll just keep this between you and Daddy." *Oh shit.*

I had planned on getting to work at eight, an hour earlier than usual. Seeing the headline about the Garbage Man killer made it impossible to concentrate on the funnies so I jumped in the shower, got dressed, and was on my way to the station by seven-thirty. I had asked Lint the day before to come in by eight, as well. He moaned and groaned a little but reluctantly agreed.

When I walked into the station Lint was at his desk with open folders lying in front of him. "Couldn't sleep at all last night," he said by way of greeting. "Been reading through these files since seven. How was your night?"

The sex was awesome! I thought, but I wouldn't be telling that to Lint. For a second I thought about my last partner, Sam Chandler, who was killed a little over a year ago. I probably would have told him about the sex. We were a lot closer. I really missed Sam.

"Jake," Lint said, "I asked you how your night was. You okay?"

"Yeah, I'm fine. Just had dinner and went to bed early."

"Me too."

I walked over to Lint's desk. "Find anything new the third time through those files?"

"Didn't find the killer's name anywhere, if that's what you're asking," Lint joked. "But I did get an address on Betty Lloyd's mother." Lint dropped the page he was reading and removed a yellow Post-it note that was stuck to his desk. "Roberta Clodfelter"

"Clodfelter?"

"Clodfelter."

Being a transplanted Yankee, certain names always struck me as comically rustic. Clodfelter sounded vaguely dirty to me. "Does Ms. Clodfelter still live in the same trailer park she lived in twenty years ago?"

"*Mrs.* Clodfelter, lives at 705 Thirteenth Avenue South."

"Nice neighborhood," I commented. I looked up at the clock. "I wonder if it's too early to pay Mrs. Clodfelter a visit."

"We could grab breakfast and *then* head over," Lint recommended.

"Breakfast is the most important meal of the day to you, isn't it, Lint?"

"Yeah … and lunch and dinner and all the snacks in between, too."

I had to laugh a little at that self-deprecating remark. Lint could be amusing, in his own fashion.

Lint grabbed a folder and handed it to me. "Here, I condensed the case down to a smaller file that we can bring with us. Thought it might be a little handier than hauling all four of these files around."

Maybe Lint didn't notice the look of total surprise on my face, but I'm sure it was there. The initiative he had taken was quite unusual. "Great Idea," I said. I decided to let him pick the breakfast spot.

*****

Lint had chosen Denny's for breakfast, which was fine with me. I had never had a bad breakfast at Denny's and today was no exception. Lint and I both had the All-American Slam breakfast, which filled me up to my nose hairs, but Lint needed an extra side of grits with cheese to fill up all his corners.

Afterwards as we made our way to the car, Lint stared across the highway at Professor Hacker's Dinosaur Adventure. "You and Bree go miniature golfing much?"

"It's been a few years. Why do you ask?"

"One of my daughters is coming home in a couple of weeks; she hasn't been home in about three years. She's gonna stay with me for a few days and then swing up to see her mother."

I opened the driver's side door and got in. "That'll be nice."

"Yeah. I gotta say, I'm a little nervous."

"Why's that?"

"I wasn't the greatest father, Jake. I was never home. We rarely did things as a family. When her mother first left me they moved over to Conway. I had visitation on the weekends. We went miniature golfing a lot; she loved it. That lasted about three years, and then her mother moved to Tennessee. I've probably only seen her about six or seven times since."

I left the parking lot and turned right on to North Kings Highway, headed toward Thirteenth Avenue. I had to admit, Lint's candidness had gotten to me. "Maybe she doesn't remember the things you do. Maybe she only remembers the good times—you and her, golfing on the weekends."

"Yeah, that's what I was hoping for. I was thinking maybe we could go again, while she was here."

"I'm sure she would like that." I took a left onto Thirteenth Avenue and started searching house numbers. When we got to 705, I turned into the driveway.

"Nice place," Lint observed.

"A long way from the trailer park," I agreed.

As we climbed out of the car Lint mumbled, "You can take the girl out of the trailer park, but you can't take the trailer park out of the girl."

I looked at him over the roof of the car. "What's that?"

"Just something my father told me once about my first wife."

"Your father told you that about your wife?"

"Yeah. On my wedding day, no less."

We walked up to the door and knocked. A woman inside hollered, "Be right there!"

The door opened, and standing before us, in a floor-length pink robe, was a very attractive woman who appeared to be in her early fifties. Her long brown hair, blue eyes, and the freckles across her nose told us immediately that this was Betty Lloyd's mother; the resemblance was remarkable. She let the door swing open and placed her right hand on her hip. In her left hand was a Bloody Mary in a hurricane glass, complete with a celery stalk and a large green olive. She sipped the drink and asked, "What can I do for you two gentlemen?"

We both pulled out our badges and Lint spoke first. "I'm Detective Avis Lint with the North Myrtle Beach Police Department, and this is Detective Jake Stellar."

"Stellar and Lint," she repeated in a most sultry tone. "One is serious and take charge, the other is chubby, and cute as hell. Together they fight crime. Sounds like a cop show."

Lint blushed at the "cute as hell" comment and asked, "We were wondering if we could ask you a few questions?"

She put up her arms and slowly turned. When she came back around she said, "36-26-36. Any other questions?" She winked at Lint. A stupid grin was plastered on his pudgy face.

I figured I'd better jump in before he got down on

one knee and proposed. "Ma'am—"

"Oh! And I was feeling so good about myself this morning … right up until you called me ma'am. My name is Roberta, my friends call me Bertie." Her eyes shot to Lint. "Would you like to be my friend?"

"Yes, Bertie." Lint managed not to bite his tongue, which was practically dragging the ground.

"May we come in … Roberta?" I asked.

She bent at the waist, stepped aside, and with an over-exaggerated wave of her hand, she motioned us in. "Yes you may."

Roberta Clodfelter led us from the foyer and down the hall to the kitchen. We took a seat at a small oak table and she turned a bar stool around to face us. Lint watched fiercely as his new friend boarded the stool and crossed her legs. When the robe slid to the side and her knee became exposed, I swear I heard him moan.

I placed the case file on the table. "Ma'am, I mean Roberta, we've reopened your daughter's investigation."

She turned and placed the hurricane glass on the counter behind her. "The Garbage Man," she said. She gazed to the right, through the sliding glass door that over-looked the pool. "That was a horrible name; it made it sound like our daughters were garbage. It sounded almost like he was doing the city a favor by taking out the trash. Betty was a good girl."

"The news outlets can be pretty cruel sometimes," Lint said, his voice faraway but sincere.

Roberta continued to stare out the window. "We were so close, Betty and I. You know, I was only fourteen when I had her. It was almost like we grew up together. Seems like only yesterday, but it was a lifetime ago." A tear ran down Roberta's cheek, and Lint jumped up and grabbed a tissue from a box on the counter. He handed it to her. She wiped away the tear and thanked him.

"Did Betty know any of the other victims?" I asked.

She turned back and grabbed her drink. "No, not as far as I know."

I read down through my own notes on Betty Lloyd that Lint had placed in the folder. "Our files said she worked at the Hard Rock Café."

"That's right."

"She got along with her coworkers?"

"She got along with everybody. Everybody loved her."

"Did she have a boyfriend at the time?" I asked.

"Not really. There was a boy she had seen a few times just before—"

"I don't remember seeing that in the file. Do you remember his name?"

"Josh … Jason, maybe. I can't remember. I had never met him, she just mentioned him a few times. They weren't boyfriend and girlfriend, or anything like that. I think maybe they had just gone to the movies a couple of times."

"Do you know if the police spoke with him?" Lint asked.

"I believe they did," Roberta replied.

In the forty-five minutes that followed, Roberta twice offered us Bloody Marys, which we declined and we asked her every generic question two veteran detectives could think of, none of which gave us answers that made us shout "A-ha!" She showed us her pool and waterfall, which she was very proud of. And she told us about her five-year marriage to the love of her life, Garvin Clodfelter, who had died of a stroke, six years ago. Garvin, as she told it, left her with nothing to worry about … ever.

When she showed us the portrait of Garvin that hung over the fireplace in the formal dining room, Lint almost swallowed his tongue. Based on looks alone, Garvin Clodfelter and Avis Lint could have been long-lost brothers.

As we got to the door, Lint said, "It was very nice meeting you, Bertie."

She took his hand and said, "It was very nice to meet you too, Avis. You're a wonderful, beautiful man." That was when *I* almost swallowed *my* tongue.

I opened the door and stepped out onto the porch. "Thank you for your time, Roberta."

She said, "You're welcome," but didn't mention *my* beauty.

When we were almost to the car, Roberta called out, "Detectives, Betty had a close friend back then, Colleen Price. Maybe she could tell you a little more than I could."

"Do you know where Ms. Price is now?" I hollered back.

"No, I haven't heard from her in years. But she used to live in an apartment on Perrin Drive."

"Thanks," I said. "We'll look her up."

Lint and I climbed back into the car and backed out of the driveway. Roberta was still watching us from the front door, and Lint gave her a fruity little wave good-bye. Roberta smiled and waved back.

"Wow, that's some woman," Lint remarked.

"Some woman," I repeated.

"I figured it up. She's sixty-four years old. She doesn't look a day over fifty."

"Figured that up in your head, eh? Didn't even use your abacus?"

"You think she's too old for me?"

"Hell no! I think a fifth wife is just what you need."

Chapter Eleven

I called Perkins on our way back to the station; he and Gwen were on their way to Coastal Carolina to speak with Paige Samuels' teachers and friends. Perkins also informed me that a DVD containing security surveillance from behind the Kangaroo Express was on my desk. He proceeded to tell me what was on the disk but I stopped him; I hate knowing the ending of a good movie.

"I didn't mean I was going to ask her to marry me," said Lint, as he walked through the door. "I just wondered if you thought I should ask her out on a date."

"You're a big boy, Avis." *a very big boy*. "That's a decision you'll have to make on your own."

"You're a big help."

I removed my weapon and placed it in the top left drawer of my desk and took a seat. I pulled my monitor over a little closer to me and inserted the DVD into the disk drive. I pressed play and then fast-forwarded it to the approximate time we thought Paige Samuels' body was placed in the dumpster.

It was another five or six minutes before I saw Paige's blue, 2010 Ford Focus come into view. You could only see the front end of the car as it made a left off of Outrigger Road and entered the Krispy Kreme parking lot. I continued to watch for another twenty minutes, fast-forwarding every so often. The vehicle never came into view again, which told me the driver exited the parking lot a few feet further north, and then took a right onto Outrigger.

Perkins had checked with other businesses in the area, but they either had no cameras facing the direction we wanted, or they had no cameras at all.

I stared at the screen for a few seconds and then watched the DVD two more times. Funny thing about a movie, no matter how many times you watch it, the ending is always the same.

I glanced up from my monitor to see Lint, on the other side of the room, talking on his cell phone. First he looked concerned, then he grinned from ear to ear, and then back to concerned. When he hung up he walked to his desk and began rummaging through one of the cardboard evidence boxes he had gotten out of storage.

I got up from my desk, walked over, and asked, "What are you looking for?"

"That was Bertie on the phone."

"Bertie?"

"Mrs. Clodfelter."

"Oh, yeah, right. What did she want?"

"She wondered if we had come across Betty's diary when we were going through the old files. I told her no."

I craned my head over the evidence box. "It's not in there anywhere?"

"No, but I told her if we stumbled on it, we would surely get it back to her."

"You know, Lint, you're a wonderful, beautiful man."

He grinned as he removed a wad of documents from the box. "So I've been told."

I walked back to my desk and ejected the DVD. "Lint, see if you can get an address on Betty's friend, Colleen Price."

"Will do."

"I'm going to call Mrs. Clodfelter back and—"

"I'll call her," Lint cut in.

"Okay, you call her back."

"Why?"

"Ask her who removed Betty's diary from the house. Ask her if anything else was taken, and if so, did she get those articles back."

"Okay." Lint pulled out his cell phone and went into the lounge.

I heard the door open behind me and turned to look. It was Archie McNeill. "Good morning, Jake."

"Good morning, Mr. McNeill."

"Archie."

"What can I do for you, Archie?"

"I was in the area for work and I thought I would stop in and see how the investigation was going. Any new leads?"

"I can't really discuss an ongoing investigation with you, Archie."

"I understand. I just wondered if you had spoken with any of the other parents. I've kept tabs on them through the years; their current addresses are in the file I gave you. Also, Monica Thomas, the black girl, she had a boyfriend at the time—Timothy Roscoe. He went to jail a few months after the Lloyd girl was found murdered; he was in for about two years. After he got out, he moved up north somewhere, Albany New York, I think. I always thought he was a likely suspect. Maybe you could check and see if there were any homicides in the Albany area that match our unsubs MO." He paused and added, "Y'all use the term unsub, right?"

"Yeah, but we usually just say unknown subject."

Wow, Un-sub, MO, someone has been spending an awful lot of their nights watching Criminal Minds. "We'll look into it, Archie."

"Thanks, Jake. It's all right there in my file. I better get back to work." He looked around the room slowly, turned, and left.

Lint returned to the room just as McNeill exited. "Was that Archie McNeill, PI?" he joked.

"Yeah. Poor bastard."

"What did he want this time?"

"He said Monica Thomas had a boyfriend, Timothy Roscoe, who did a stint in jail on an unrelated charge after the killings occurred. He said the guy moved up to Albany after he got out."

Lint thought a moment, piano playing his lips with his fingertips. "Didn't see anything in McPherson's notes about that, either."

"Look this Roscoe character up. Find out if he did move to Albany. If he did, find out if there were ever any murders that match our subject's MO."

"Good idea."

"It wasn't mine. Did you get an address on Colleen Price?"

"Not yet."

"What are you waiting for?"

"I just got off the phone with Bertie."

"And?"

"She said besides the diary, the police took some jewelry, one of those pre-paid flip phones, and a laptop computer. She got everything back except for the diary."

"Does she still have the phone or laptop?"

"She said, no. She got rid of most of Betty's things when she moved into the new house."

"That diary would be a nice thing to have, right now. Get that address, and I'll buy you lunch at Duffy's."

Funny how fast Lint could move when there's food involved.

Chapter Twelve

Colleen Price lived in the upstairs apartment of a duplex on Perrin Drive in Crescent Beach. It was obvious the downstairs apartment was empty and appeared to be unlivable, due to the broken windows, no curtains, and the smashed in front door.

Judging by the amount of toys scattered about within the confines of the four-foot high, unpainted picket fence, Colleen had a lot of children.

Lint opened the gate and I scanned the yard for a dog—a surprise I don't like. Satisfied that I wouldn't be mauled to death by whatever they considered a family pet, I entered. We wove a pathway through a swing set, various toys, an old refrigerator, a picnic table, and a small kiddie pool that contained a green, slimy, water-like substance.

"Care for a swim?" I asked Lint as we passed the pool.

He glanced down at the contents and shuddered. "No thanks."

We climbed the staircase to the front door and knocked. We could hear children inside, but no one came to the door, so I knocked again.

"What now?" a woman screeched from inside. "Get the goddamn door!"

Lint and I looked at each other. "Maybe we came at a bad time," Lint said.

"Maybe we should have called first," I added.

The door opened and a small shirtless child poked his head through the opening. "What do y'all want?" he asked somberly.

Lint bent down to talk to the little fella. "Is your mommy at home?"

"No," the tot answered. His blonde hair was uncombed, and he was sporting a red Kool-Aid mustache.

"Where is she?"

"At work."

"Is there a grown-up here?"

"Yes. Ms. Colleen."

"May we speak with Ms. Colleen?" Lint asked patiently.

The boy pulled his head back inside and slammed the door. A few seconds later we heard a woman shout. "Well, who is it?"

There was a pause and then she hollered, "Well,

what do they want?" The next thing she shouted was, "Jesus Christ!" and then the door opened. A disheveled woman in ratty pajama bottoms and an ancient Lynyrd Skynyrd concert T regarded us suspiciously with her scarecrow arms folded across her skinny braless chest. I thought for a moment she was wearing Billy Bob novelty teeth but realized with a depressing jolt that they were hers. I wouldn't have been surprised if she cooked a little meth on the side.

"Colleen Price?" Lint asked.

"Who wants to know?" was her reply. A different child tried to poke his head through the door and Colleen pushed him back with her foot. "Get back inside, goddammit."

"I'm Detective Stellar and this is Detective Lint; we're with the North Myrtle Beach Police Department," I announced. "We were wondering if we could ask you a few questions."

She rolled her eyes and let out a loud sigh. "I told the other cop that I haven't seen him in two weeks, and whatever he's done, it ain't got nothing to do with me."

"Whatever *who's* done?" Lint prompted her.

"Frankie. Isn't that why you're here?"

A child inside hollered for Ms. Colleen, but she ignored her.

"We don't know anything about Frankie, ma'am," Lint replied. "We're here about Betty Lloyd."

For a second Colleen looked as though she had

seen a ghost but quickly regained her composure. "Well, I sure as hell haven't seen her; she died, like, twenty years ago, or something."

"We know," Lint informed her.

"Why was the other officer looking for Frankie?" I asked.

"None of your business! I don't have time for this." She slammed the door.

Lint and I looked at each other and then back at the door. "She don't have time for this," Lint mocked.

I looked over the railing into the yard full of old and broken toys. "She better make time," I said, and reached down to turn the knob; she had locked it. I gave the door three hard raps with the side of my fist. When she didn't answer I did it again.

Colleen yanked the door open. "What now?"

"Are you running a daycare center here, Ms. Price?" I asked.

She sighed again. "I watch some kids. There's no crime against that."

"There is, if you don't have a license to *operate* a daycare center."

"Oh, great! Now you're going to harass me for trying to make a living."

"Ms. Price, why don't you step out here and answer some questions for us, or we will have this place shut down for good—within the hour."

A small, teary-eyed boy tugged on her dingy pajama bottoms. "Ms. Colleen, Billy keeps pushing me."

"Yeah, well I'm going to push you even harder if you don't get your ass back in front of the TV like I told you. Jesus Christ, you little bastards are more trouble than you're worth." Colleen stepped out on to the deck and shut the door behind her. "Now, what do you want?"

I didn't hide my disgust. "Ma'am, I could run you in for suspicion of child cruelty. Now, I suggest you ditch the attitude and cooperate, unless you want my partner and me to search the premises for whatever might be in there."

Colleen fell silent. Her scared expression said she would be a good girl.

"We were told by Betty Lloyd's mother that you and Betty were very good friends at one time," I said.

"Yeah. We both grew up in that goddamn trailer park. I got out of there and never looked back."

"You've come a long way," Lint commented.

"Mrs. Clodfelter told us there was a boy Betty had dated a few times. She said his name was Jason or Justin. Do you remember a boy by that name?"

She threw her head back and laughed, showing her missing, broken, and blackened teeth. "Remember Justin? Hell, I married him."

"You married your best friend's boyfriend?" Lint asked.

"He wasn't her boyfriend. They dated a few

times, but she wouldn't put out—she had her head so far up that other guy's butt—so Justin came sniffin' around me."

"And you helped him with his problem?" Lint asked.

"You know I did. Justin was somethin' back then. Real good lookin'. Like a cross between Patrick Swayze and Dog the Bounty Hunter."

Lint nodded his head. "Yes, that would be one good-lookin' man."

"Are you still married to him?" I asked.

"Hell no! He dumped me a year after we got hitched. Said I wasn't *good* enough for him."

"Go figure," Lint said.

"I know, right?"

"Where is Justin now?" I asked.

"Who knows? I haven't seen him since the day he walked out. I been with Frankie for eight years now."

"Frankie's last name?" I asked.

"Barnes."

"Whatever happened to the other guy?" I asked.

"What other guy?"

"The one whose butt she had her head so far up," Lint responded.

"Oh, him. Never knew his name," Colleen replied. "Betty was all hush-hush about it—didn't even tell her mom about him."

"She say where she met him?" Lint asked.

"Um … I remember she said she met him at work one night. She worked at the Hard Rock back then. I think he might have worked there too, if I remember right. Like I said, she kept quiet about it."

"Thank you for your time, Ms. Price," I said as Lint and I started down the stairs.

She leaned over the railing, her saggy goat-like tits aimed at us like twin torpedoes. "Hey, why are you asking about Betty, anyway?"

Lint stopped and turned. "We think the guy who killed her is back in town. Rumor is he's come back to tie up any loose ends."

"Oh my God!"

When we got back in the car I turned to Lint and asked, "Why the hell did you say that?"

"I hate her, and I thought maybe it would scare her."

I laughed. "Yeah, she's no Bertie, is she?"

Lint got a dreamy look on his face. "No, she sure as hell ain't."

Chapter Thirteen

"So you don't think she's too old for me?" Lint asked as we walked through the door and into the squad room.

"I don't think it would be a problem, especially since you look ten years older than her," I answered. I walked over and stowed my weapon in my desk drawer. Gwen and Perkins were both at their desks.

"Yeah, you're probably right, she wouldn't want anything to do with me."

"That's not what I meant, Lint."

"Who looks too old for whom?" Perkins asked.

"No one," Lint shot back.

I laughed. "I don't think he wants to discuss it."

"Lint, you old horn dog, so you've got a new girlfriend?" Gwen needled him.

"No, Gwen," Lint replied slowly. "Do you have a new boyfriend you would like to discuss?"

Gwen's face went white. "N-n-no," she stuttered. "What makes you ask that?"

"No reason," Lint said. He walked over to the coffee pot and poured himself a cup. "Coffee, Jake?"

I glanced over at the mud he was pouring into his cup. "I'll pass."

"Didn't get much at the school," Perkins offered. "Paige's teachers liked her, classmates liked her. She was a hard worker, no enemies."

I ejected the DVD from my computer and placed in back in the case. "Nothing on here that helps." I tossed the case onto my desk.

Perkins leaned back in his chair, stretched his arms toward the ceiling, and then clasped his fingers behind his head. "What's next?"

"I need you to hunt down a Timothy Roscoe," I said. "He dated Monica Thomas around the time of her death and went to jail shortly after the Lloyd girl's body was found."

Perkins jotted down the name Timothy Roscoe on a piece of paper. "Sounds like a good lead. I don't remember seeing his name in McPherson's notes."

"McPherson seems to have left a *few* things out of his notes," Lint agreed.

"Archie McNeill gave us Roscoe's name, said he heard Roscoe moved up to Albany after he got out of prison," I told Perkins. "Check any unsolved murders in the Albany area that might have our same MO."

Perkins began typing away at his keyboard.

"Gwen," I said, "I need you to do something for me."

"Sure. What?"

"See what you can dig up on one Frankie Barnes. Also, run a check on Colleen Price. Lint and I went to see her today over on Perrin Drive. Looks like she's running an illegal daycare out of her house. Nasty place, vile woman with meth teeth. Might be cookin' the stuff."

Gwen nodded and began punching her keyboard.

"What's next for us?" Lint asked.

I didn't answer him right away, because I didn't know what was next. Things weren't really coming together. I wished I had Betty Lloyd's diary; I was sure there was something in that diary that I needed to know. McPherson knew what was in there, but he wasn't talking.

I cracked my knuckles in frustration. "Who knows?" I answered.

Lint shrugged his shoulders as he got up from his desk. "I gotta make a phone call," he said. The moment the words left his mouth, his cell phone rang. He shot me a surprised look and then answered his phone. "Hello? Oh, hello, Bertie." He raised his brow and grinned. "I have no plans. What time is good for you? Okay, I'll see you at seven." He hung up his phone and slipped in back into his pocket.

"Good news?" I asked. Gwen and Perkins were staring bemusedly at the rotund Romeo.

When Lint realized what had just taken place, the grin slowly left his face and was quickly replaced by a look of fear. "She wants me to come over for coffee at seven."

"That's great!" I said.

Lint motioned for me to follow him out to the parking lot. When we reached a secluded spot he bent over with his hands on his knees, breathing heavily and vigorously shaking his head "no" like a mad billy goat. "What am I going to do?" he asked miserably.

"About what?"

"She wants me to come over for coffee. What am I gonna do?"

"Go over for coffee."

"I can't go over there." Lint raised his arm and pointed back at himself. "Look at me!"

"What's wrong with you?"

"I'm fat."

"I know."

"I can't go to a woman's house looking like this."

"You were at her house this morning, and maybe you didn't realize it at the time, but you were really fat then, too."

"This isn't a joke, Jake."

"I'm not making a joke. What I'm trying to say is, she already knows you're fat and she invited you over to her house anyway. She seems to like you even *though* you're fat. Not to mention, you're practically a dead ringer for her dead husband."

Lint's breathing began to slow, and he wiped the sweat from his forehead. "Yeah, maybe you're right."

"I am right." We stood there silent for a few more minutes as he calmed down. "You okay, now?"

"I think so."

"Good. Let's head back inside, it's hot out here."

I turned and started for the door, when Lint grabbed my arm. "Wait!"

"What now?"

"What if she wants to have sex?"

"You have kids by four different women, Avis; I'm sure you know how to have sex."

"But when I take off my clothes, I'm even fatter … and hairier."

"Stop worrying. She knows how old you are, she knows how fat you are. Trust me, she knows what to expect. Besides, you saw that portrait of her late husband; he was fat too. Obviously she seems to like fat men."

"You're right … you're right. I'm being stupid."

"I know." Lint walked ahead of me and I slapped him on his fat sweaty back. "And in the future, never describe your naked, fat, hairy, sweaty body to me ever again."

"I didn't mention sweaty," Lint recalled.

"I know, but that's my point. Someone takes one look at you with clothes *on* and they immediately know exactly what to expect when you're naked; so does Bertie."

Lint cocked his head. "That makes me feel a little better … just a little."

Chapter Fourteen

"How was work?" I asked, as I got undressed.

"Good," Bree answered. "*Almost* uneventful."

"Almost?"

"There was an accident out on Highway 50 this morning; two vehicles were involved, they hit head on."

"I heard something about it on the radio. Everyone okay?"

"No. The driver of the car was killed. Only nineteen years old. The passenger, his girlfriend, had some minor injuries. The guy driving the truck was airlifted to Charleston."

The only thing I could think to say was, "That's too bad."

"How was your day?" Bree asked.

"Good." As I walked down the hall, naked, toward my bathroom, I hollered back over my shoulder, "Lint met a woman today."

"What! What do you mean, *met a woman*?" Bree hurried down the hall behind me.

I pulled back the shower curtain and turned on the water. "He has a date."

"When?"

I climbed into the shower and closed the curtain. "If you get in here with me, I'll tell you the rest of the story."

She ignored my request. "Where did he meet her?"

"Can't hear ya; waters too loud. Maybe you better step in here with me."

"I don't want to get my hair wet."

"Put on some water-proof underwear."

"*Very* funny, ya pig."

I was happily surprised when the shower curtain opened and Bree stepped in. "Yowza!" was the only romantic thing I could think of to say.

Bree smiled shyly, moved in close, and put her arms around me. "Glad I can still evoke a yowza."

"You're evoking more than just a yowza," I informed her.

"Calm down and finish your story."

"Turn around and I'll rub your shoulders," I offered. She did as I asked and the second my thumbs pressed into her back she let out a quiet moan. *Story time is over*.

*****

We had moved from the shower to the bed at some point. I was lying on my back with my fingers clasped behind my head. Bree lay on her side; her head on my chest. I looked over to my right at the million-dollar dog, who was now sitting in the doorway staring at me. She was probably angry about what I had just done to Mommy.

Bree was sound asleep and it was only six-thirty. I was starving. "Hey," whispered. She didn't move. I would like to think that I had worn her out with my sexual prowess, but I knew it probably the long workday at the hospital.

"Hey," I said again, this time a little louder.

"What?" she yawned.

"I'm starving."

"Me too."

"What are you making for dinner?"

"Reservations."

"Where?"

"Wherever you want."

"Chinese?"

"No."

"Ryan's?"

"Naw."

"You said anything I wanted," I reminded her.

"Yeah, anything is fine."

"You pick."

"You never finished the story about Lint's date."

I told her the entire story while we got dressed. While she did her hair and makeup, I probably could have told her the entire story of *War and Peace*, but instead I went into the living room and turned on the television. I stopped on MeTV and began watching an old episode of *M*A*S*H*. I reached down and picked up the dog, which had followed me into the living room. I sat down in my recliner, and placed the dog on my lap. "You want to watch some TV with Daddy?" I asked in a silly voice.

"What did you just say?" Bree shouted from her bathroom.

"Nothing."

"Did I just hear you call yourself, Daddy?"

Oh crap! "No. I said, 'Do you want to watch some TV *laddie.*'"

"Sure you did. Woofie's a girl, remember."

Shit! "Just hurry up, I'm starving." I pulled the handle on the La-Z-Boy and reclined. Woofie wiggled into place between my legs and placed her chin on my knee, ready to watch *M*A*S*H*.

I immediately rolled my eyes when I discovered it was the episode called *Who Knew?* I sat and watched Hawkeye read through the diary of a nurse he'd briefly dated, Lt. Millie Carpenter, and discovered she'd had feelings for him before she died. I thought, H*ow convenient.* I wished Father Mulcahy would stop by with Betty Lloyd's diary.

Bree stuck her head into the living room. "Ready?"

"Ready."

Woofie jumped from my lap to the floor and ran to Bree. She danced around in a circle on her hind legs.

"Look how cute she is," Bree squealed, and bent down to pet her.

"Yup," I answered, as I climbed out of my recliner. "She's something."

"Sorry, Woofie, you can't come with us."

I grabbed Bree's keys off of the counter as I walked through the kitchen toward the door to the garage. I looked back and Bree was still fussing over the dog. "You coming?"

"Yeah, yeah, I'm coming. We have to stop for gas. I'm on E."

"Ugh!"

Chapter Fifteen

It was around ten o'clock Wednesday morning as I drove the unmarked cruiser along North Kings Highway toward the Windy Hill area of North Myrtle Beach. Lint had just asked me what I had done the night before, a question he now routinely asked me every day without fail. I remembered back to the good old days when Sam Chandler was my partner, before he was murdered. Every morning he, too, would ask me what Bree and I had done the night before. The only difference was, after I answered Sam, I would then ask him, with genuine interest, how his evening was. I rarely asked Lint about his night, mostly because I didn't give a shit. I knew he wanted to tell me about his big date with Roberta Clodfelter, and he was chomping at the bit for me to ask.

"We just went out for a late dinner," I answered.

"Where'd you go?" Lint asked.

"Russell's, over in Murrell's Inlet. It's a seafood place." I took a left onto Windy Hill Road.

"Is it right on the Marsh Walk?"

"No. It's across the street," I said. "But we did take a walk along the water after dinner."

"That's nice," Lint commented as he gazed out the passenger side window.

I knew he was waiting for me to ask, so I did, with precision timing. "What did you do last night?"

"Oh, I went over to—"

"Hold that thought," I said and pulled to the side of the street. "We're here." I climbed out of the car quickly to make sure he *had* to hold that thought.

As I walked around the car, I glanced over my shoulder. Irma Lambert, the woman we had spoken with on Sunday, was in her front yard raking up some small dead branches. When she saw me, she stopped raking and gave me the thumbs up. I guess the gesture was to inform me that Jean McPherson was now home. Just for the hell of it, I returned the thumbs up. She smiled and winked conspiratorially. Irma obviously thought we were partners now.

Lint led the way up the stairs to the second floor of the McPherson home and knocked on the door. "Mrs. McPherson?" he asked when the door opened.

"Yes," said Jean McPherson. "What can I do for you gentlemen?"

"I'm Detective Lint, this is Detective Stellar," Lint answered, displaying his gold shield. "We were wondering if we could come in and ask you a few question, ma'am."

"What is this about? There was concern in the seventy-something woman's voice.

"It's about a case your husband worked in the mid-nineties," I informed her.

"Ray? Why, he's been dead almost twenty years."

"We know," I responded. "May we come in?"

Jean pulled the door open a little farther and motioned us in. We entered into the kitchen and she pointed toward the table. "Have a seat, detectives. Can I offer you a cup of coffee? It's fresh."

I said, "No thank you," but Lint accepted and scanned the room. I'm sure he was looking for a freshly baked goodie.

The coffee's aroma as she sat a mugful in front of Lint made me regret my decision. *Why do I do that?*

Jean pulled out the chair across from me and to Lint's left. "So, what's this about an old case of my husband's?"

Lint was blowing into his mug to cool the coffee, but paused to ask, "Haven't you seen the news since you returned home?"

"I got in late last night, and I haven't had the television on yet today; my show isn't on until one."

"*Days of Our Lives?*" Lint asked.

"It's the only one I watch now."

"I love that sh—"

I quickly interrupted Lint. "Mrs. McPherson—"

"Call me Jean."

"Jean, do you remember a case your husband was working on in '95? Four yo—"

"Oh, my goodness!" Jean exclaimed. "The Garbage Man, those poor girls."

"That's the case," said Lint.

I nodded solemnly in agreement "Yes, ma'am, the Garbage Man."

"But, why … what questions would you have for me?"

"Jean, we think he may have resurfaced," I told her.

"That's impossible. I mean, after all these years … how? I don't understand." Jean got up from the table and walked to the cupboard and grabbed a cup for herself. As she filled it she asked, "Are you sure I can't pour you some coffee, Detective?"

I foolishly declined again. I wonder what a psychiatrist would say about this compulsion of mine.

When Jean returned to the table she sat with her pale, veiny hands wrapped around the cup as though she was trying to keep them warm. "You know something, detectives? For twenty-three years, every time my husband walked out that door and went to work, I wondered if he would be coming home that night. But every night he came home, and with him came his job. When he finally retired, I thought, now things will change, now I can relax. Eight months later he was out back mowing the lawn and dropped like a sack of shit, clutching his chest."

I smiled at Jean's earthy choice of words as she demurely sipped her coffee.

"Your neighbors said the two of you fought a lot," Lint blurted out.

I shot him a look.

Jean smiled. "I didn't say I cared if he came home, I just wondered if he would."

Lint chuckled, and then apologized for the chuckle.

Jean put up her hand. "It's fine. He was a real son of a bitch."

"Did he ever discuss the case with you?" I inquired.

"No, he never discussed much of anything with me. I'll tell you one thing, though, the worse the case he was working, the bigger prick he was, and he was a real asshole during this whole Garbage Man thing."

"Did he leave any personal files behind when he passed, perhaps things he worked on at home?"

Jean snorted. "The only thing he worked on at home was a bottle of Jack Daniels." She pointed a boney finger over my shoulder. "See that bottle of Jack on the shelf over the fridge?"

I looked back. "Yeah."

"Been sittin' there since the day he died. Whenever I feel a bit nostalgic, and think I might miss him just a little bit, I glance over at that bottle and it cures me of that foolish notion."

"But you say he didn't keep any personal files of unsolved cases he had worked on?" Lint pressed.

Jean shrugged. "There were papers in his desk and file cabinet in his office. I didn't look through any of it, just boxed it up and stuck it, along with anything else of his, right in the garage."

"Would you mind if we took a look in his things, Jean?" I asked.

"Help yourself." She pointed down the hall behind Lint. "The hall leads to stairs that go down to the garage. After you're done you can leave through the garage door; just lock up when you leave."

We thanked her, got up from the table, and headed for the stairs. As we made our way down the hall I noticed that there were many family photographs hanging on the wall, but none of Ray McPherson.

There were boxes and boxes of Ray's things stacked against the back wall of the garage. It was as if Ray's entire life had been erased from his castle, and banished to the dungeon. The boxes contained the framed photographs that probably hung in the hall when he was alive. We found several ash trays, as well as an unopened pack of Lucky Strike. There were several old issues of Playboy and Penthouse, which had Lint asking, "I wonder if these are worth anything?"

"Who knows?" was my answer. I laid them aside.

Lint pulled the lid off of a small cardboard box and looked inside. "Check this out!" he said.

I looked inside. There were four folders; each

one had the word "unsolved" scribbled on the front. We went through each file. One was a murder case from eighty-one. Another was from eighty-five—a string of home invasions. The other two files were from ninety-on both child abductions. The abductions didn't seem to be related to each other.

"Well, now we know he kept personal files," I said.

"All but the one we're looking for," Lint sighed.

I lifted the back of my jacket and slid the files into my waistband. "I think I'll take these with us." I put the lid back on the box and put it back where Lint found it.

We spent a good hour and a half searching through the boxes, but there was nothing else of any use to us. The only thing we really learned about Ray McPherson, that we didn't already know, was that he loved to fish. There were several photographs of him and a young man we figured was Ray Jr., on shore and in a rowboat, with fishing poles in their hands. Many of the photos showed father and son grinning from ear to ear as they held up the catch of the day by a metal stringer.

When we left, we locked the door behind us.

Chapter Sixteen

We were almost back to the station when my cell phone rang. "Stellar," I answered.

"Jake, it's Perkins. Where you at?"

"On our way back to the station. What's up?"

"Might have something. I'll fill you in when you get here." He hung up.

I hoped he had something, because we sure didn't. I pushed the accelerator a little closer to the floor.

As Lint and I walked through the squad room door Perkins was already walking toward us. He had an excited grin on his face. We met at my desk and he handed me his cell phone. "What's this?" I asked. I glanced over at Gwen, seated at her desk. She dropped the pen she was writing with and leaned back in her chair.

"Hit the call button,' Perkins said. "It's Archie McNeill's number."

I played along. After I hit "call" I put it up to my ear. You've reached the voice mail of Archie McNeil. Leave your name and number and I'll get back to you as quick as I can. If this is an emergency, please call Carolina Security at 1-888-555-1423 for faster service.

"I don't get it," I said.

"I made some calls," said Perkins. "Carolina Security. That's the company that installed and services the security equipment at Krispy Kreme."

I handed Perkins his phone. "So, McNeill knows which cameras weren't operating."

"Exactly!" Perkins said.

"But what reason would McNeill have for killing Paige Samuels?" Lint asked.

Gwen spoke up. "Think about it. McNeill has suffered this loss for twenty years; he even ended up in a psychiatric ward over it. The man lost everything. He kills Paige Samuels in the exact same way as his daughter was killed and the case gets reopened. All he's ever wanted was answers. What better way to get them?"

"That's why Paige wasn't sexually assaulted," Perkins added. "He couldn't do that. He's a murderer, not a rapist."

"Let's pick him up," I said.

Perkins shook his head. "Why don't we just wait till he calls back? I left him a message when *I* called.

Told him I needed to ask him a few questions about the case. I'll just have him come in."

"Sounds good," I agreed. "Just make sure nothing spooks him. We don't want him running." I started toward Merle's office. "I'll bring the captain up to speed."

"What do you want me to do?" Lint asked.

"What can ya do?" I joked. Lint didn't think it was funny, but Gwen and Perkins laughed. Probably kind of prickish on my part, so as I walked away I threw in a "No offense."

"None taken," Lint grumbled.

I stopped. "Did anyone get back to you from Albany?"

"No," Lint answered. "I'll give them another call."

"Good idea," I said and went into Merle's office.

"What's the good word?" Merle asked.

"Perkins and Gwen like Archie McNeill for the Samuels murder," I answered.

"Why?"

I explained their theory to the captain and it sounded good to him as well. I told Merle we were waiting for McNeill to get back to us, rather than hunting him down. Merle agreed it was a good idea but looked at the clock over the sofa and added, "If you don't hear from him by five, go get him."

I said, "With pleasure," and then filled him in on the Jean McPherson interview.

As I walked out of Merle's office, Lint looked up from his desk. "Nothing in Albany," he said. "I got a hold of the detective I spoke with yesterday. He said nothing matching our guys MO came up in the Albany or Schenectady area. He also looked up Monica Thomas' old boyfriend, Timothy Roscoe. He owns a small home improvement business in Colonie, a suburb of Albany. He hasn't been in any trouble at all since his release from prison."

"Sounds like a model citizen," I said and then looked to Perkins. "Nothing from McNeill?"

"Not yet," said Perkins.

"We go pick him up if we don't hear back from him by five," I said.

"You got it," Perkins said, and picked up the phone on his desk. "I'll set it up just in case."

My eyes went back to Lint. "Lunch?"

His face lit up. "Thought you'd never ask."

I led the way out the door. "Come on, you can tell me all about your date last night."

Lint shook his head and shot me a sly grin. "I knew you were dying to hear about it."

I would rather *die than hear about it*, I thought. "I sure was," I said diplomatically.

Chapter Seventeen

Lint and I sat at a small metal table in front of Sonic. I was surprised that he only ordered two hotdogs. He also got a small order of fries and topped it all off with a diet soda. I wondered if last night's rendezvous prompted a sudden urge to lose weight.

I bit into my cheeseburger and savored the taste before asking, "So, how did it go last night?"

Lint took a sip of his drink. "She baked an apple pie."

"Was that the highlight of the evening?"

"No, I was just mentioning it."

"How late did you stay?" I asked. "Or did you stay the night?"

"I didn't stay the night, I left around eleven."

For someone so eager to talk about their evening, this was like pulling teeth. After every answer I waited for more, but soon figured out I would have to keep the questions coming. "What did you do all night?"

"We talked. We sat by the pool and had coffee and pie. She makes a great pie."

"There's the pie again."

"Jake, it was a really good pie!"

"I guess it was."

"We watched TV for a while. She likes a lot of the same television shows I do. We like a lot of the same music too."

"It's good to have a lot of things in common. You can't base an entire relationship on pie."

"She has a camp too—on Lake Marion. She likes to fish, and she has a boat."

"Pie, camp, and boat. Sounds like the perfect woman."

"She is, Jake. She's perfect."

"Did you make plans to see each other again?"

"We're supposed to go to dinner Saturday night."

"Where are you going?"

"I haven't decided. Where should I take a woman like her?"

"You mean a woman who makes great pie and likes to fish?"

"No! A woman who's wealthy. Where do you take a rich woman for dinner?"

"Lint, if she really is perfect, she won't give a shit where you take her for dinner."

"I guess you're right. I have a few days to decide, anyway." He took a bite of his hotdog and washed it down with soda. "It really was a great night."

"At least you didn't have to get naked."

"I *did* give her a goodnight kiss," he said cunningly.

"Attaboy," I said. "Not to change the subject, but do you have Roger Grayson's phone number in your cell?"

"No, but it's in the file in the car," Lint answered, getting up from the table. "I'll grab it." When he returned with the folder he reached inside and pulled out a list of names and numbers; Grayson's name was halfway down the list. "Here ya go."

"Thanks," I said, pulling out my cell phone.

"What are you thinking?"

"Something you mentioned about the camp and fishing got me thinking." I dialed the phone.

"Yeah?" came Grayson's grumbly voice from the earpiece.

"Roger, it's Jake Stellar."

"What did you forget?"

"Nothing. I was just wondering something."

"And what would that be?"

"When we were at McPherson's widow's house this morning we came across a bunch of old photographs of him and his son fishing. I noticed the fishing poles on your porch. Did you and him ever fish together?"

"We sure did. Many times. Me, him, and that boy of his went up to the camp and fished a couple times a month."

"Do you still own the camp?" I asked.

"Oh, it wasn't my camp," Grayson explained. "That was Ray's camp."

"Do you know if Ray's wife still owns the camp?"

"No, he left that camp to the boy in the will. That's R.J.'s place now."

"When was the last time you were up there?"

"I haven't been there since Ray died."

"Where's it located?"

"Lake Moultrie."

I said, "Thanks, Roger," and hung up the phone.

"You're thinking Ray may have left some paperwork or files at the camp." Lint stated.

"Sure am."

"We'll never get a warrant."

"I know. Maybe we should give Ray Jr. a call."

We got up from the table and dumped our trays. On the way to the car, Lint said. "Speaking of camps, Bertie said she goes up to her camp for the weekend every year at the end of October."

"Oh, yeah?"

"Yeah, she wants me to come up with her."

"Oh, yeah?"

"Yeah. And I was thinking maybe you and Bree could come too."

"That would be great," I lied.

*****

When we arrived back at the station Gwen and Perkins were out to lunch. Lint and I went in to tell Merle about the camp that Ray McPherson Jr.'s father had left him, but before we could tell him, he said, "Lint, you got a call from a Special Agent Sam Burrows at the FBI Headquarters in Nashville. Something about a search you asked them to do on our subjects MO." Merle slid a note pad across the desk in Lint's direction. "Here's his number."

Lint grabbed the notepad and hurried to his desk. I walked over to the window that divided Merle's office from the squad room. With my index finger, I lifted one of the slats in the blinds and peered out. Lint was already seated at his desk and dialing the phone.

I turned and told Merle about McPherson's fishing camp on Lake Moultrie. I told him about the missing diary, and about Ray McPherson's missing files on the case.

"You'll never get a warrant based on that," was his reply.

Lint burst through the door. "Guess what?"

Merle shot me a look and then glared at Lint. "I'm not playing a friggin guessing game. What is it?"

I chuckled a little.

"Got two hits on the MO." Lint began reading from his notes. "Back in 2000, in Kingston Springs, Tennessee, a twenty-two year old girl was abducted while walking to a friend's house. The next morning her body was discovered by a janitor in a dumpster behind the elementary school. She had been raped and beaten to death; her eyes were tapped open with duct tape. Then, in 2005 in the town of Dickson, Tennessee, a twenty-five year old woman disappeared somewhere between her home and the church where she played the organ. Her body was found two days later in a dumpster behind a Pilot Travel Center; she had been raped and murdered. The coroner's report said an unknown sticky substance had been poured into her eyes before her death. Here's where it gets good." Lint paused for dramatic effect. "Ray McPherson Jr. lives in Nashville. He has worked for Country Courier since 1999. Country Courier transports medical and financial files for banks and hospitals. I checked—Junior makes the Nashville to Memphis run twice a week, along I-40. Kingston Springs, Dickson, and the Pilot truck stop are all along I-40."

"That'll get you a warrant," Merle said. "I'll get in touch with state and local PD and set it up. You two round up Perkins and Gwen, I want Archie McNeill brought in now."

Chapter Eighteen

Archie McNeill rented a trailer on Kingfisher Street in the Creekside Mobile Home Park—the same trailer park where Betty Lloyd and her mother, Roberta, once lived. Lint and I were in one unmarked unit and Perkins and Gwen were in another. We went in with no lights or sirens and pulled up in front of Archie's trailer. Lint carried the search warrant and the arrest warrant in his inside jacket pocket. In his left hand was a pry bar.

I had my hand on my weapon, but left it in its holster as I walked up the path to Archie's door. Gwen stayed near the street with her weapon drawn at her side. Perkins positioned himself at the rear of the trailer with the back entrance in his line of sight. I stood on one side of the front door and Lint on the other.

I knocked three times, loudly, and hollered, "Archie McNeill! It's Detective Stellar, with the

North Myrtle Beach Police Department," I waited a few seconds and knocked again. When there was no answer I nodded to Lint and drew my weapon. Out of the corner of my eye I could see Perkins draw his weapon as well.

With both hands, Lint jammed the pry bar between the door and the doorjamb, a few inches above the doorknob. With all of his strength, he pushed the bar and the door popped open.

I was first through the door, with Lint close behind. "Archie McNeill!" I shouted once more.

Archie McNeill wasn't home. His house was spotless. There were no dirty dishes in the sink, and none drying on the rack. His bed was made, and two pairs of his shoes were sitting neatly on the floor by the door. His floors had been mopped and the living room carpet had been vacuumed. There was a faint smell of lemon in the air. On the kitchen table was a sheet of loose-leaf notebook paper, and on it Archie had made a list:

CALL TO HAVE ELECTRICITY TURNED OFF

CANCEL NEWSPAPER

HAVE MAIL STOPPED

TURN OFF CABLE

Next to the list was a note that read:

Jake,

I knew it wouldn't take you long to figure out that it was I who killed Paige Samuels, and put the body in the dumpster. It was a horrible thing to do, I know, but I felt it was my only option. I needed the case to be reopened. For the longest time I had faith that my daughter would one day be returned to me alive, but, over time, as my faith dwindled, I became desperate. I know you will find my Mary's killer and bring him to justice. I am going home now to be with my family.

Thanks,

Archie McNeill

Lint and I, along with Gwen and Perkins, were on our way to the house on Madison Drive when the call came in. After writing the note, Archie drove Paige Samuel's car to Madison Drive, back to the house he once shared with his wife, Tamara, and his daughter, Mary. When the current owner returned home that evening from work, he found Archie McNeill in the garage, hanging from the same truss his wife had hanged herself from years earlier.

Chapter Nineteen

I pulled into my driveway that night and hit the button on the garage door opener. When the door lifted and I drove into the garage, I couldn't help but think about Archie McNeill hanging from the ceiling of his old garage.

McNeill had kicked in the front door of the house and helped himself to a ham sandwich and a glass of milk before going into the garage. The homeowner stated that when he arrived home, the television was on and the half empty glass of milk sat on an end table next to the recliner. He said he went out to the garage to retrieve a baseball bat to use as a weapon in case the intruder was still in the home; that's when he found Archie hanging from a length of clothesline rope, suspended above an overturned step ladder. He also informed the coroner that he knew immediately that Archie was dead, judging by the color of his face. It didn't take the coroner long to confirm this fact.

The garage door was open when Lint and I pulled up in front of the house. I was glad that someone had already taken Archie down and placed him in a body bag. When I saw the body bag lying on the gurney my first thought was: *There but for the grace of God go I.*

I knew what it was like to lose a child. Bree and I had lost our son Ricky in a car accident when he was barely six years old. There's not a day that goes by that I don't think of him. What would he be doing now? What classes would he be taking in his first year of college? Would he have girlfriend? It seems like a thousand similar questions come to mind every day.

A part of me wishes I had met Archie McNeill a week earlier. I could have told him about Ricky. Maybe he just needed someone to talk to. I could have told him how I spent a few years trying to drink myself to death. I could have told him that it always hurts but that it does get a little better. Maybe it would have saved Paige Samuels' life. But, by the time I met Archie it was too late. Even if he didn't kill himself, he would have spent the rest of his life in prison.

I pressed the button and closed the garage door behind me. When I got in the house I took off my jacket and hung it on the back of one of the kitchen chairs and kicked off my shoes. I rolled up my sleeves as I walked through the living room and out to the pool. I carried my phone with me.

"Hey," Bree said. She was sitting in the pool, on the steps, throwing a small green ball across the yard for the dog to chase.

"Hey," I said back.

"How was work?"

My throat was dry and my voice cracked a little when I replied, "Not good."

"You want to talk about it?" Bree's voice was always so calm and soft when she knew something was wrong.

I sat in one of the patio chairs. "Not really."

She got out of the pool and I tossed her the towel that was crumpled on the table next to me.

I glanced over at Woofie—God I'll never get used to that name. The expression on his face said that he was wondering why the game of fetch had ended. I had never owned a dog in my life, and was amazed that an animal could have such a distinctive personality. He lay down next to the ball and dropped his head into the grass.

Bree dried off and walked over and sat in the chair across from me. "Is there anything I can do?"

"Pour me a glass of Scotch."

"Other than that?"

"No." She noticed my cell phone lying on the table. "Expecting a call?"

"Yeah. Waiting for a judge to sign a warrant. Thought we would have it by now."

"What's the hold up?"

"It's out of our jurisdiction. Merle is setting things up with the state and local PD."

"Where is it?"

"It's a camp on Lake Moultrie."

"Oh, that's beautiful up there. I always wanted to rent a place up there for a week; right on the lake."

I grinned for the first time since I had been home. "Funny you should mention that."

Bree cocked her head. "What do you mean?"

"Turns out Lint's new lady friend has a camp on Lake Marion, and it's been mentioned that you and I might be invited up there next month."

"That would be great!"

"Would it? I don't know if I could spend a week in the same camp as Lint."

"You spend almost every day together," Bree pointed out, as though *that* would somehow make it better.

"Yeah, I know. But when I work with him, I get to come home every night without him. If we vacationed together I would have no escape."

"Maybe if you got to know him a little better, you would get along a little better."

"Or, maybe not."

Bree shrugged off my fear of being with Lint 24/7 and informed me, "We'll cross that bridge when we come to it." I don't think she realized I was going to spend the next few weeks worrying about crossing that bridge.

"Uh-huh," I mumbled.

"So, what's she like?" Bree asked.

"Who, Lint's … whatever she is?"

"Yeah. Would I like her?"

"You like everyone, so, probably."

"I don't like everybody," she snapped back.

"What about your friend Aida and her husband Luca?"

"They're really nice."

"See what I mean? She's annoying as hell and he goes to the gym every day and thinks he's a ninja. They're not nice—they're weird, both of them. And what about Doug and Katie, across the street?"

"What about them? They're nice people."

I rolled my eyes and threw my head back. "Oh my God! *She's* sleeping with the guy that mows their lawn, and *he's* banging his secretary."

Bree glared at me. "And you gossip worse than an old lady."

"I'm just trying to point out that you think everyone is great, everyone is nice. It's like your color blind, but instead of not being able to see colors, you can't see when someone is an asshole. You're *asshole* blind!"

"So? I would rather *like* everyone than *hate* everyone, like you do. Just because you deal with some of the worst people doesn't mean you have to dislike everyone." Bree got up from the table and walked toward the door, opened it, and turned back toward me. "Believe me," she said through clenched teeth, "I'm not asshole blind, because I can see you." She went in and slammed the door behind her.

The second that door shut was the same second I realized that she was right: I was an asshole. I had just taken one of Bree's best qualities and turned it into a something bad. Why do I do that? Why do I bring home my horrible day and pile it on top of her, especially when she has probably had a bad day of her own?

I glanced over at the dog again. With the look he was giving me, I was glad Woofie couldn't speak; she'd probably call me an asshole, too.

I got up from the table and went in to apologize, and the dog followed me in. As I reached our bedroom door and saw Bree lying on the bed, my cell phone rang. She heard it, too, and turned her head toward me.

"Yeah," I said.

It was Merle. "Get back here. We got the warrant."

"Be right there."

I hung up, walked over, and sat on the bed. "I'm sorry for that. It was a bad day, but I shouldn't have taken it out on you."

Bree sat up in bed, put her arms around my neck, and laid her head on my shoulder. "I knew you were a dick when I married you," she joked. At least I think it was a joke.

"I love you," I said.

"I love you, too. Was that Merle?"

"Yeah. I gotta go." I kissed her on the forehead.

She took my head in her hands, pulled me closer, and kissed me on the lips. "Be careful."

I kissed her one more time and stood up. "I'm always careful. I'll probably be pretty late. Don't wait up."

"I won't be able to sleep."

"I'll call you as soon as it's over." I reached down, picked up Woofie, and sat her on the bed next to Bree. "At least you'll have company."

Chapter Twenty

It was almost a two and a half hour drive to Moultrie Lake, and Lint never shut up once. By the time we reached the turn-off I knew everything I ever wanted to know, and didn't want to know, about Avis Lint. For example: I didn't know that he had a large mole on his left ass cheek that usually became infected if he rode in a car for more than two hours.

We traveled along Route 6 until we saw the State Trooper cruiser on the side of the road, where they said they would meet us. I pulled to the side of the road and we got out. As I approached the car, the driver rolled down his window.

"You guys been waiting long?" I asked.

"About fifteen minutes."

I held out my hand. "Jake Stellar." The trooper shook my hand through the window; I turned toward Lint. "This is Avis Lint." When I looked back Lint was scratching his ass cheek vigorously. *I should have brought Perkins*, I thought.

"Bobby Collins," the driver introduced himself, and then nodded toward his partner. "Jason Black."

I nodded to the other trooper.

Collins handed me some paperwork. "Here's the warrant."

"Thanks."

"You want us to ride in with you?" Collins asked. "It's about a mile down this dirt road."

"Sure, if ya don't mind," I answered.

Lint and I climbed back into our car and followed Collins and Black down the dark winding road. There wasn't a cloud in the sky, and the full moon lit up the night, enabling us to approach with our lights off. At the speed we were traveling it felt more like three miles than one. We passed two other camps in the first five hundred yards, but that was it for the rest of the way.

At the end of the road we drove into a clearing, with the camp on the left, and followed the driveway around a flagpole and parked in front of the modest log cabin.

"Did you see that?" Lint asked.

"See what?"

"I thought I saw a light inside when we pulled up."

I looked past Lint, out through the passenger window at the old place. "It's just your imagination.

There's flashlights in the trunk."

Collins and Black met us at the trunk of our car. "Jason said he thought he saw a light inside when we drove up," Collins said.

"I told ya!" Lint blurt crowed.

I lifted the trunk, reached in, and grabbed the two flashlights. I handed one of them to Lint, along with the warrant. "Here ya go. Go knock on the door and see if anyone is home," I said, just to bust his balls a little.

Collins laughed.

"I'm not walking up there by myself," Lint protested.

"A big strong cop like you, with a gun—what do you have to be afraid of?"

Collins was still grinning and Black snatched the warrant out of Lint's hand. "Give me that for Chrissakes," he said. "I'll do it."

Black started up the walkway toward the front door and Lint followed close behind, still scratching his ass.

"I wasn't scared," I heard Lint say, more to himself than anybody else. "I'm just not used to the woods."

Collins leaned closer to me and whispered, "Why's he keep scratching his ass like that?"

No sooner than I got out the words "Infected mole" than we heard glass shatter and the flash of two shotgun blasts lit up the surrounding area.

The first shot hit Black in the chest, lifting his feet off the ground and driving him backwards. He landed on his back in front of Collins and me. The second shot hit Lint in the right shoulder, spinning him into the dirt like a top. I hit the ground on my belly and scooted sideways under the rear of the car, behind the tire. I looked to my right and Collins was on the ground too. I had my 9mm out and Collins' revolver was in his hand and pointing at the house.

I whispered loudly to Collins, "You hit?"

"No."

"Lint!" I called out at the same volume.

"I think I'm okay, Jake. Got me in the arm. Hurts like hell."

"Don't move," I said.

"Jason!" Collins said. There was no answer. "Son of a bitch! They said no one was here."

My cell phone began to vibrate and I answered. "Yeah?"

It was Perkins. "Hey. Just got a call from Nashville PD. Ray McPherson Jr. had a delivery in Knoxville this morning. A buddy called him and told him the cops were looking for him. That was this afternoon; he hasn't been heard from or seen since."

"Think we found him. Notify the State Police that we have shots fired and two officers down."

"Shit!" Perkins shouted. "I'll get a hold of them. Stay on the line."

I said I couldn't and hung up just as another slug hit the side of our car.

I turned to Collins. "I'll keep Junior busy, you drag Jason behind the car." I fired five shots into the cabin's broken window as Collins jumped to his feet. He grabbed Jason by the collar with both hands and ran backwards behind their cruiser.

Collins ripped open Jason's shirt. "It doesn't look like it went through his vest," he shouted. "I've got a pulse."

Collins turned, rose up, and began firing over the hood of their vehicle. I jumped up and ran to Lint. He was bleeding badly and was now unconscious. I took hold of his hand and dragged the big man behind our car.

When we were out of the line of fire I knelt down beside him. I smacked his cheek a few times. "Avis," I said. "Open your eyes, buddy." The trunk was still open. I stood and grabbed a blanket and the first-aid kit. Collins fired into the house a few more times.

I tore open Lint's shirt and placed all the gauze in the kit over his wound and then wrapped it as tightly as I could with an Ace bandage. I slapped him again, a little harder this time and he opened his eyes. "Stay with me."

"I don't like the woods," he whispered. I spread the blanket over him.

"Try to stay awake," I told him.

"My daughter's coming home," he said.

"I know."

"I don't want to die."

"You're going to be fine." His eye lids fluttered

and closed again. I pulled out my weapon again and turned toward the building. "Ray!" I shouted. "Don't make this any worse than it is! Lay down your weapon and come out."

Ray shouted back, "How can it get any worse?" and then fired two more times, neither round hitting anything.

He was right, it couldn't get much worse. He had murdered at least six women and had now shot two police officers. "It could get a lot worse, Ray. You're coming out of that cabin alive, or dead—you chose," I hollered. Collins fired two more times at the window.

The last thing I wanted was to kill Ray McPherson Jr. A dead man couldn't tell us where Mary McNeill's body was.

"I'm not afraid to die!" Ray shouted.

"What about your mother, Ray? She doesn't want her son dead." He didn't answer, so I yelled, "Where is Mary McNeill's body?"

"Why should I tell you?"

I heard movement to my right and glanced over. Jason Black was coming to; he was moaning and holding his chest. I looked down at Lint; he was still out.

"You smell smoke?" Collins asked.

I looked up; smoke was beginning to rise out of the chimney. I knew he was burning whatever files his father had kept there, maybe even Betty Lloyd's diary. "We gotta go in," I said.

"How do you want to do this?"

"You start firing at the windows and don't stop. I'm going through the front door."

Collins reloaded and took aim over the hood of his vehicle and began firing.

I took off running as fast as I could, and hit the front door with my shoulder just as Collins fired his fifth shot. The doorjamb splintered and the door flew open. I hit the floor and rolled over to my knees.

Ray Jr. was in front of the fireplace; he spun around and froze. The only light in the room was from the fire he was building and a flashlight that lay on a table next to him. In his hand were documents and a small book. Leaning against the table was his shotgun.

"Don't move, Ray."

His arm moved toward the fire, as he stared into my eyes.

"Don't do it."

I could hear Collins coming in from behind me. He came through the door slowly and moved around to my left; his weapon trained on Ray.

"Don't do anything stupid," Collins said.

Ray tossed the papers into the fire and then lunged toward his shotgun.

Collins fired twice, once into Ray's abdomen and once into his chest. I fired once into his chest. He smashed into the table, breaking two of its legs, and hit the floor. The upset flashlight fell next to him, spinning for a moment and casting crazy shapes on the walls of the cabin.

I ran to the fireplace and began pulling burning papers from the fire. I placed them on the floor next to me and patted out the embers with the palm of my hand. When I finished I walked over to Ray and got down on my knees next to him.

"Where's Mary McNeill's body?" I demanded.

Rays eyes were rolling back in his head. I shook him and shouted, "Where is she!"

His voice was quiet and raspy. "My father and I buried her out back."

I shook him again. "Why didn't your father turn you in?"

"He killed Betty Lloyd, not me."

"Why?"

"He brought her up here, and they caught me."

"Caught you with Mary?"

"Yes. He had to kill Betty so she wouldn't say anything."

Ray McPherson Jr.'s eyes rolled back one final time and closed.

I picked up Betty Lloyd's diary and the rest of the papers. As Collins and I walked out on to the porch we could hear the wailing of sirens off in the distance.

Chapter Twenty-One

Around eleven the following morning, Bree and I walked into Lint's hospital room. Behind my back I had a take-out bag from Sonic.

Roberta Clodfelter was standing beside Lint's bed holding his hand.

"Jake!" he chirped, as we walked in.

Roberta turned toward us and smiled. "Jake Stellar, thanks for bandaging up my man."

"All in a day's work," I said.

Bree walked around to the other side of the bed and sat her pocketbook on a chair. "How are you feeling, Avis?"

Lint let out a melodramatic groan. "Pretty sore. Bree, this is my friend Bertie Clodfelter. Bertie, Bree Stellar."

They shook hands and Bree said, "Nice to meet you."

"It's nice to meet you, too. Avis has told me so much about you."

"How they treating you?" I asked.

"Good," Lint answered. "But the food is crap."

I pulled the bag out from behind me and sat it on his belly. "Maybe this will help."

"Oh, wow! Thanks, guys," he said, and fumbled to open the bag with one hand.

"Let me get that for you," Roberta said, opening the bag and pulling out one of the two hotdogs.

"They said Ray Jr. didn't make it." Lint said.

"He was pronounced dead at the scene," I told him.

"The trooper was okay, though?"

"Yeah. Three broken ribs, but he'll be fine."

"That's good."

"When are they letting you out of here?"

"Day after tomorrow, they said."

"The doctor said he would probably be out of work for a month," Roberta commanded. "I was thinking about bringing him up to my cabin for a few weeks to recoup. Nothing like the great outdoors to cure what's ailing you."

"That'll be nice," Lint said. "I love the woods."

"I heard that about you," I joked. I turned to

Roberta. "Oh, I have something for you too."

Bree turned and pulled the diary from her purse and handed it to Roberta.

"It's your daughter's diary," I said.

Roberta took the diary, looked it over, and placed it against her heart. "Oh, my goodness. I didn't think I would ever see this again." She looked at me. "Did you read it?"

"Yes. It turns out she met Detective McPherson at work one night; she was tending bar. They saw each other for a few weeks. She didn't tell anyone because he was married. Her last entry was on the morning she disappeared. She wrote that Ray was bringing her up to his cabin for the weekend."

Roberta stared quietly at the floor for a second and then asked, "Did they find the other girl's body?"

"Yes. Ray and his son buried her behind the cabin. She'll be laid to rest in a plot her father bought between him and her mother."

"That's good." She looked from me to Lint. "I had given up on my daughter's killer ever being brought to justice. Thank you both."

We stayed and visited for a few more minutes. Before we left, Roberta invited Bree and me up to the camp. I glanced at Lint, saw the eagerness on his face, and said, "That would be great."

The End

COMING SPRING 2016
From Here to There
Six Short Stories

COMING SUMMER 2016
Most Likely to Die
From the Tales of Dan Coast

ALSO BY RODNEY RIESEL

Sleeping Dogs Lie

From the Tales of Dan Coast

A mystery set in the Florida Keys follows Dan Coast, an unlicensed private detective of sorts, as he is hired to find the missing boyfriend of a woman who herself soon ends up missing. When someone from the woman's past unexpectedly shows up at Dan's home, with a story of faked deaths and missing life insurance money; Dan along with his sidekick Red set out to find the money, and the woman.

ISBN: 978-0-9883503-0-4

Ocean Floors

From the Tales of Dan Coast

The second installment in the Dan Coast series, Ocean Floors, is a tale of mystery and possible romance when a chance meeting with a beautiful young woman leads Dan and his trusted sidekick Red down a road of murder and kidnapping. Join Dan and Red as they try to solve the murder while searching for a missing friend.

ISBN: 978-0-9894877-0-2

Impaled

An Adirondack Short Story

Eric Stone is an investigator with The Town of Webb Police Department. Chuck Little is Head Ranger at the Nick's Lake campground. An unlikely duo, together they work to solve a murder that mimics a spree of gruesome murders taking place years earlier. Is it a copycat, or has the murderer resurfaced after all of these years? Join Stone and Little as they piece together the clues to solve this mystery taking place in the small village of Old Forge in the Adirondack Mountains.

North Murder Beach

A Jake Stellar Novel

The first installment of the story of North Myrtle Beach police detective, Jake Stellar. The spring bike rallies have ended, the spring breakers have all gone back to school, and the summer tourist season is a few weeks away. What better time for a police officer to take a nice quiet relaxing week off from work? That's what Jake Stellar had in mind. That is until someone from his past resurfaces to remind him of a terrible secret he has spent years trying to forget. In North Murder Beach, a story of revenge, Jake is unwillingly and violently forced to confront his secret from his past.

ISBN: 978-0-9894877-1-9

The Coast of Christmas Past

From the Tales of Dan Coast

Coast of Christmas Past is the third book in the Dan Coast series of books. Dan Coast is all set to spend Christmas just the same way he has every year for the past few years; alone and drunk. But when uninvited, unexpected guests arrive and throw a wrench into his holiday plans he is forced to sober up (slightly), and throw on a smile. Just when it seems nothing else could go wrong, a close friend is injured in what appears, to the police, to be a drug deal gone bad. Dan Coast and his sidekick, Red jump into action to find the truth while their friend lies unconscious in the hospital.

ISBN: 978-0-9894877-3-3

The Man in Room Number Four

The Dunquin Cove Series

When a mysterious stranger arrives in the small coastal town of Dunquin Cove, Maine it appears as though Claire and her young son, Mica's prayers have been answer.

But who is he, and why is he really here? Join Claire and her guests at the Colsome House Bed and Breakfast as they piece together the mystery of the Man in Room Number Four.

ISBN: 978-0-9894877-2-6

Ship of Fools

From the Tales of Dan Coast

Ship of Fools is the fourth book in The Tales of Dan Coast series and begins where Coasts of Christmas Past left off. Find out how Dan deals with the death of a young friend, while looking into the disappearance of a new friend's sister. Join Dan, Red, and Skip as they fumble their way through a new mystery.

ISBN: 978-0-9894877-4-0

Beach Shoot

A Jake Stellar Series

It's a beautiful Sunday morning in North Myrtle Beach and Emily Bowen, a wife and mother of four, lies dying on the beach. Jake Stellar returns in Beach Shoot, a new mystery by Rodney Riesel.

Beach Shoot is the second Jake Stellar book and sequel to the Amazon Best Seller North Murder Beach. In Beach Shoot, Jake finds himself teamed up with the most unlikely of partners, his nemesis and fellow detective Avis Lint. Join Jake and Avis as they piece together the clues in this thrilling new mystery.

ISBN: 978-0-9894877-5-7

Return to Dunquin Cove

The Dunquin Cove Series

It's been almost six months since the day ex-hitman, Ben Dunning turned up in Dunquin Cove, Maine, not knowing where or who he was. He's lived a quiet, peaceful life in the small town, but now his old life is calling him back. As Ben plans a trip to Boston in search of his past, little does he know that trouble is brewing in Dunquin Cove. Two strangers have arrived with the promise of safety and security. Join Ben and the people of Dunquin Cove as they band together to prove they can take care of themselves and their town.

ISBN: 978-0-9894877-7-1

Double Trouble

From the Tales of Dan Coast

Shortly after Walter and Warren Bowman arrive in Key West in search of a sister they never knew they had, Warren disappears. With nowhere else to turn, Walter enlists the help of Dan Coast. Join Dan as he and sidekick Red Baxter search for the missing Bowman family members, while dealing with the fallout of an ongoing case.

ISBN: 978-0-9894877-9-5